I0552036

Richard Carpenter's

ROBIN OF SHERWOOD

THE SERVANT

Richard Carpenter's Robin of Sherwood
The Servant
Written by Jennifer Ash

First published in 2021
(as part of the Series 4 Collection)

This new edition
Published in 2024 by
Chinbeard Books

in association with
Oak Tree Books
oaktreebooks.uk

Editor: Barnaby Eaton-Jones
Range Consultant: Harriet Whitehouse

Robin of Sherwood TV Series
created by Richard Carpenter
Copyright © 1983 HTV/Goldcrest Films & TV

The right of Jennifer Ash to be identified as the
author of this work has been asserted in accordance
with the Copyright, Designs and Patents Act 1988.

All rights reserved. No reproduction, copy or transmission
of this publication may be made without express prior
written permission. No paragraph of this publication may be
reproduced, copied or transmitted except with express prior
written permission or in accordance with the provisions of the
Copyright Act 1956 (as amended). Any person who commits
any unauthorised act in relation to this publication may be
liable to criminal prosecution and civil claims for damage.

This book is a work of fiction and, except in the
case of historical fact, any resemblance to actual
persons, living or dead, is purely coincidental.

Richard Carpenter's

ROBIN OF SHERWOOD

THE SERVANT

by
Jennifer Ash

A Chinbeard Books / Oak Tree Books Original

Richard Carpenter's

ROBIN OF SHERWOOD

THE SERVANT

by

Jennifer Ash

PROLOGUE

Robin sat bolt upright, the gesture stirring him from a deep sleep. His eyes wide, he felt a surge of hope; a hope that died as reality greeted him with Sherwood's dawn chorus of singing bird's and Tuck's snoring.

He knew it was irrational to feel cheated when she hadn't been there; ready to embrace him as he woke—and yet he couldn't help it. Robin bit back a groan. This was the third night in a row he'd had the same dream.

Her voice had been so clear that Robin's unconscious self had been convinced he'd only need to open his eyes to be able to see and touch her again.

'Your father will come round, you'll see. Have strength. You'll need it when they come. But it will be alright. I'll be there for both of you.'

Pulling his hood over his head, Robin lay on his side with a sigh. Reaching out an arm to embrace Marion's sleeping form, he closed his eyes to try and recapture the feeling of safety his night-time thoughts had given him. But it was no good. The vision of Mathilda of Huntingdon had gone.

What will be alright, Mother? Who is it that's coming?

CHAPTER 1

Even though the castle walls threw out enough shadow to make a man doubt what he saw, there was nothing to impair the hearing of anyone passing along the stepped corridor. Jerrard knew he hadn't misheard the words which leaked through the open door of Sir Guy of Gisburne's quarters. He wished he had.

Blowing out the candle he held, Jerrard felt the cold invade his ageing bones as he listened to the nearby conversation. He could hear Flynn, the captain of the sheriff's guard, as clearly as if he'd been stood right beside him.

'Your return from France stifled my prospects, Sir Guy. I don't see why I shouldn't be compensated for that fact.'

'Compensated!' Sir Guy's reply was venomous.

'For doing my job so badly, the sheriff threw you aside like a chicken bone in favour of Jonas! Then, when I walked back through the castle gates, he didn't give either you or him a second glance! You only hold the post of captain now because Jonas got himself killed.'

'The sheriff was amazed you survived the battlefield.' Flynn snapped back, 'and you're only here because I was sent to drag you back from Gisburne village after your so-called marriage! Although why the sheriff wanted you back after you disgraced yourself so, I'm at a loss to think!'

Hoping that no one else would walk that way, Jerrard froze against the stone as he weighed up whether he should run up or down the staircase when his eavesdropping was over.

'You will regret saying that!' The sound of Gisburne's palm connecting sharply with the soldier's face made Jerrard wince, but Flynn didn't so much as whimper.

'You speak to me of regrets? Curiously fitting, Sir Guy, when *you* should be the one to regret your actions. Regret leaving that piece of black and yellow cloth lying around for Jonas to find, and pass to me. Regret allowing me to witness you parading around your room in that tunic you think you'd hidden in

4

your trunk. A tunic with a similar black and yellow design. A man should shut his door at night. What do you think the sheriff would do if he learned of such a garment's existence within his castle's walls?'

'You've been spying on me!'

'No, I have merely been paying attention.'

Jerrard heard the rapid draw and clash of knife on knife; but only once. A single scrape of metal and the dull thud of wrists thumping together. He imagined Flynn staring at Gisburne over the paired blades as he spoke.

'The sheriff is not a stupid man, my Lord. He has noticed an increased surliness and contempt in your manner that's greater even than your usual level of scorn. He bid me keep an eye on you.'

Gisburne muttered, 'De Rainault is a fool, One day soon he'll…'

'He is less of a fool than you think!' Flynn cut across Guy's threats. 'However, I have no intention of telling him what I've seen. I know what that tunic means, but if you want to prevent your secret reaching the king, then I suggest you put that dagger away and pay me enough marks to make sure I don't get talkative.'

Gisburne scoffed, 'You threaten me, yet you

have no understanding of what is coming! Of what I might become!'

'Sir Guy,' Flynn's voice dripped with forced patience, as if he was admonishing a stubborn child. 'I threaten you in the knowledge that you'll get what all bullies get in the end. Nothing.'

Even though he couldn't see Sir Guy, Jerrard could picture his face. Round, pink; screwed up in contorted anger, as he spat his reply. 'It is *you* and every soul in this cursed castle that will be nothing! You wait, you'll see. They are coming. They are *all* coming!'

Jerrard hardly dare breathe. He wanted to move, but he stayed still. He was paid to listen, and so he listened.

No more words came from the chamber. But as he strained his ears, Jerrard fancied he heard the sheathing of knives and the clatter of coins into an outstretched palm. Seconds later Flynn appeared in the doorway.

'A wise decision, Sir Guy. I advise you to think carefully about what you are doing. No man can serve two masters.'

Jerrard put a hand over his mouth to muffle the sound of his breathing as Sir Guy slammed the door in Flynn's face.

Weighing the coins in his hand, Flynn ran down the stone-stepped corridor, passing Jerrard without stopping. The servant wasn't sure if he had been seen and his presence dismissed as unimportant, or if Flynn hadn't noticed him at all. It didn't matter. Jerrard had other things to worry about.

Lying still and silent on his cot at the side of the castle's great hall, separated from the vast space by nothing more than a run of tapestries, Jerrard felt his palms prickle as he listened to his fellow servants grunt and snore in their sleep.

Clenching his hands into tight fists, he relaxed them again, but still his palms tingled. It was a sign he'd learned not to ignore—albeit the hard way. A smile flitted across his troubled countenance as Jerrard thought of his former mistress. It had been so long ago and yet he could hear her now, telling him for the umpteenth time that the tingle of tension in his hands was his body was trying to tell him something and that he should respect it enough to listen.

I'm not sure I want to believe what I'm thinking this time, Mathilda. Please God, I'm wrong. And as I have no proof, just theories, then I might well be in error. But you taught me I should always trust my instincts.

He closed his eyes. If his suspicions were right, then the implications for Nottingham could be severe.

But it wasn't that fear which sent dots of perspiration across the old man's forehead as he watched a spider dance a fresh web across the tapestry to his left.

If I'm right Mathilda, then it isn't just the sheriff's position in jeopardy, but all of England. Jerrard concentrated, trying to work out what it was about the overheard conversation that had made him especially fearful.

"They are coming. They are all coming". And they talked of a tunic—a hidden tunic. A man only hides his colours if he's ashamed of them or...

A fresh image of Mathilda, her head tilted up, her back straight, a bow and quiver full of arrows slung carelessly over her back as she strode through the forest behind Huntingdon castle, came to mind. He could hear her as if she was there, sat on the wooden stool at his side. 'A man hides his colours if he is a coward or an enemy infiltrator waiting for the right moment to strike. Often such men are one and the same.'

Jerrard shivered. *The Knights of the Apocalypse.*

The order of fighting men, all of noble birth, had been the source of gossip and rumour for months. Some claimed that it dated back for decades. Many dismissed the order as mythical, but Jerrard wasn't so sure.

Gisburne wouldn't be that stupid—would he?

Even as the thought crossed his mind, Jerrard knew he would. A minor knight who lived his adulthood as if trying to prove something to a cruel, long dead, father.

Of course he would.

Each week bought new murmurs and uncertainty. The Knights of the Apocalypse were causing waves of anxiety across England. There were whisperings of noblemen's sons going missing. Even Pope Innocent seemed affected. The fact that Rome was on the verge of ordering an Interdict had certainly unsettled Abbot Hugo. When it went ahead, then sanctions over England's churches would be imposed, leading to the closing of churches and the suspension of religious ceremonies.

If these knights are affecting the Pope... Jerrard frowned into the dark. *Or is it a co-incidence that there's talk of an Interdict now, just as this supposedly religious order, grows stronger?*

The old man grunted. It wasn't a co-incidence. He remembered King Richard's crusades. To his mind, they achieved no more than to teach future generations how to use religion as a political weapon to steal land and goods that belonged to people in foreign lands, as well as at home.

9

Again his mind flew to Mathilda. They'd talked often about the harm King Richard was doing to his people; daring to hope that, for all his faults, John would be better. It was to prove to a futile hope. And then Mathilda had died and Jerrard had been sent to Nottingham by her husband, the Earl of Huntingdon. At first his role had been to act as the earl's spy and to report the sheriff's misdeeds; from false accounting to excessive cruelty. Then, in time, his duties had expanded, and he was entrusted to keep an eye on de Rainault's plans for the earl's son.

'Master Robert.' Jerrard grinned as he thought of how the mischievous boy had been able to wrap him around his little finger. It had been hard leaving him in Huntingdon when the earl had first assigned him to Nottingham, but his friends Aland and Edgar had watched over the boy well enough. Even though Mathilda's son had no idea of his role in his life, Jerrard took comfort in listening out for the worst of the sheriff's excesses, so should Robert need his help, it would be received.

Jerrard sighed. That had been his plan anyway; yet he couldn't always get word to Huntingdon about the sheriff's and Gisburne's latest scheme. He hated that his instructions from Huntingdon had been to watch, but not interfere. Robert had, in the earl's words, "chosen his own path, and he must walk it alone." But that didn't mean the earl didn't worry about his only son.

Only son.

Jerrard felt his palms prick again. If Gisburne was involved with these knights, even if there was the tiniest chance their power would unmask the earl's biggest secret, he couldn't let that happen. He'd sworn…

Why do I think that? How could they possibly find out when Gisburne doesn't know?

Swinging his legs over the side of the cot, Jerrard rubbed his short beard as he looked around. No one stirred.

You know where you have to go. Trust your instincts. Trust your loyalty. Find Robert.

Jerrard froze. They hadn't been his thoughts— had they?

Shaking his head, he pulled his scrip from beneath his cot, stuffed in his only change of clothes, took up his water pouch, mercifully already full, and his knife. Then, wrapping his cloak around his shoulders, Jerrard got up, surveying the place that had been his home for almost fifteen years. He had no idea if he'd ever come back.

Knowing it was impossible to avoid being seen by at least a handful of people, for a castle never truly sleeps, Jerrard made for the kitchen. Grabbing some bread, he left a message to say, should his absence be noted, that he'd been called to Papplewick, to tend a sick relative.

By the time he'd crossed the drawbridge and was making his way towards the road to Sherwood, dawn has risen. Lost in thought, for the first time in years, Jerrard did not take care to see if anyone saw him go.

Flynn glowered as the figure slipped out of the castle. He was sure it was the same man who'd be lurking in the shadows when he'd left Sir Guy. He hadn't been able to put a name to him then, but now if came to him.

Jerrard.

'Where are you going so early old man?' Flynn's hand went to his sword. 'And more importantly, how much did you hear me say to Gisburne?'

Following for a while, the captain paused as he watched the servant turn, not along the road towards Newark, or towards the crossroads that ultimately led south to London, but into the forest.

Flynn hurried forward, wondering what it was that was taking Jerrard to Sherwood, and what it was he knew...

CHAPTER 2

Perched on a branch halfway up a tree, Much's legs swung to-and-fro. He held his bow and arrow at the ready. He couldn't see Nasir, which probably meant the Saracen was really close.

They'd been stalking deer through Sherwood since dawn; Nasir tracking and Much beating and acting as lookout. Now, at last, they'd cornered one.

Drawing back his bowstring, Much paused and listened. As soon as he heard the sound he'd been waiting for—the faint warble of Nasir's bird call through the trees—Much fired. The deer buckled to its knees, before crashing to the floor. The arrow had hit the beast cleanly, killing it fast. Much hated it if they struggled in death.

Nasir appeared from where he'd been hiding as Much landed by his side. Gesturing for his young friend to continue to keep watch, the Saracen pulled out the arrow, wiped it on the ground and passed it back to Much. Then, crouching down, he heaved the animal over his shoulders. 'Food for many here.'

Keeping his bow to hand, an arrow nocked in place, Much followed Nasir as they headed back to camp. His mouth was already watering at the thought of roasted venison, even though it'd be late evening before Tuck had cooked it.

They hadn't got far when Nasir stopped dead. A second later Much heard the noise that had caused his friend to falter. The unmistakable crack of a twig under a careless foot. Both outlaws dived under cover. Nasir slumped the deer to the ground and drew his swords. Much pulled back his bow, waiting, statue still, as the sound got closer. Nasir lifted up a hand, raising one finger, and then another. Two people. One following the other.

Much kept his bow taught. Who was being followed? And more importantly, what manner of man was trailing them—and why?

Jerrard wrapped his hand around his knife. With each step into Sherwood, he felt he was getting closer to his target and yet increasingly lost.

Once or twice he'd had the sensation that he was being followed, but whenever he'd stopped to listen he'd heard nothing but the breeze in the trees and bird's singing. Wondering if he should stop and go back, he ploughed on anyway, telling himself his imagination was getting the better of him. The forest was full of unfamiliar sounds. It was probably a rabbit or a peasant.

The path became no more than a single thin track, before it suddenly split into two walkways, one leading east and one north. Jerrard stopped, unsure which direction was most likely to take him to Robin Hood.

You're a fool. You have no idea where you're going. You could be lost for days in the forest and not see a soul.

The crack of a footfall behind him sent Jerrard scurrying east, for no other reason than, if he failed to find Robert, he might at least get back to the road and beg a lift that would eventually take him to Huntingdon.

Questioning his judgement with every new step, Jerrard plunged forward.

Why have I come here? I have no evidence that Gisburne is up to anything other than his usual ill lain plans. And if Flynn is jealous enough of his superior to risk his neck by blackmailing him, then why should I care? And yet, with each stride further into the heart of Sherwood, the servant's instincts nagged at him.

What if the Knights of the Apocalypse existed as a power far greater than gossip has speculated? What if they used sorcery? And what if Gisburne was part of that? If the earl's greatest secret was ever to be uncovered, and they got to hear of it then…

Jerrard's thoughts were abruptly cut short as a hand shot out from between the trees, clamped itself over his mouth, and dragged him off the main path.

Flynn froze midstride. Lowering his boot to the rough ground, taking care not to make a sound, he gripped the handle of his dagger tighter. All of a sudden, every tree potentially had a hidden outlaw behind it.

Had he heard a muffled shout, or had he imagined it?

So intent on stopping the servant and keeping his business with Sir Guy a profitable secret, Flynn hadn't stopped to think what the consequences of following a man into Sherwood could be.

Jerrard was just an old man. He could have dealt with him at the castle without breaking a sweat, but he'd been so lost in his thoughts, Flynn had followed the servant blindly—and in the process, hadn't noticed how far into Robin Hood's territory he'd strayed.

Flynn strained his ears; listening for any sign of life.

Nothing.

Pulling his knife from his belt, Flynn took comfort from its presence. He crept on, wondering if Jerrard was looking for the outlaw or had simply opted to use Sherwood as a shortcut to one of the forest villages.

Nasir put a finger to his lips, indicating that their guest should be quiet.

Much lowered his hand from the old man's face with a mouthed 'sorry.'

Jerrard, his pulse racing, gave a curt nod as he recognised his friendly kidnappers. Staying still alongside his unexpected helpers, he held his breath as Flynn appeared, his cloak billowing around covering his captain's uniform.

Listening to each footfall, for one terrifying second, Jerrard had been sure that the soldier had looked right at him as he'd peered into the undergrowth on either side of the track, and yet he'd walked by their hiding place as if there had been no one there.

It was only when Flynn had been out of sight for a tense few minutes that the Saracen lowered his finger from his lips. 'He's gone.'

Much let out an exhalation of air in a hearty puff. 'Hello, I'm…'

'You're Much and he's Nasir.' Jerrard gave a short bow. 'I'm honoured to meet you at last. Thank you for helping me.'

Much looked at Nasir, who shrugged.

'After all these years, you can't imagine there to be many folk in Nottingham who don't know who you are, surely?' Jerrard gestured to the fallen deer. 'Would you like a hand carrying that to Robert? I may be old, but I'm strong enough to pull my weight.'

'You look for Robin Hood?' Nasir's eyes narrowed, not missing the use of "Robert" rather than "Robin".

'What do want 'im for?' Much peeped out of their hiding place, double checking there was no sign of trouble. 'And why was the sheriff's captain following you?'

Nasir cut in, 'And who are you?'

Jerrard held his hands up as if to stem the flow of questions. 'I am looking for Master Robert—sorry, Robin Hood. Flynn, that's the captain's name, he doesn't know that's why I'm in Sherwood. I'm as certain as I can be that he was following me because I overheard something I shouldn't have.' The old man scrubbed at his chin as he rested back against a birch tree, speaking to himself as well as his companions. 'I didn't think he'd seen me listening, but he must have.'

'Your name?' Nasir persisted.

'Jerrard. I am—or perhaps was—a servant at Nottingham castle.'

Nasir bent down, hoisting the deer back onto his shoulders. 'This way.'

Much, his bow still in hand, smiled at their visitor, but years of living as an outlaw in the forest meant, despite his inclination to be welcoming, he remained suspicious. 'You are a friend, aren't you?'

'I am.' Jerrard nodded, 'but you are wise to be wary. Should de Rainault have discovered who I really am, then he'd surely revel in using me as a lure in one of his traps to capture you and your leader. However, he does *not* know, and I am not part of any plot against you.' He smiled, 'I can't prove that of course.'

'What do you mean, who you *really* are? And why did you call him Robert and not Robin?' Much pushed back some branches so Nasir could pass along the path with their dinner over his back.

'Because that's how I know him. He was just a little boy when I last saw him. Eight years old and running his father ragged.'

19

Much's eyebrows rose. 'You knew Robin when he was a child?'

'I served his mother back then, and I serve his father now.'

Nasir paused to adjust the weight of the deer, 'You're a spy in the castle.' He spoke, not as if asking a question or as if making an accusation, but merely as one stating a fact.

'Yes.' Jerrard met the Saracen's gaze, unblinking. He knew what a bad reputation most spies had. Often well deserved. 'And I have news for the Earl of Huntingdon and his son. Urgent news which, I am very much afraid, neither of them will be able to do anything about.'

CHAPTER 3

Nasir threw the deer to the ground about two hundred yards from the camp and looked straight at Much, 'Go ahead. Tell Robin we have a guest.'

'But we're almost there, we…'

Jerrard dipped his head in approval. 'Nasir is suggesting you tell Robert I am with you. Mention my name and I'm sure he'll come. No need to give away where your camp is unless you have to.'

As Much dashed forward without another word. Nasir bowed, 'Forgive my caution.'

'Caution is something I respect and understand.' Glad to rest his feet a while, Jerrard perched on a fallen trunk, stretching his weary limbs out before him. 'I'm assuming you learned such instincts the hard way. You fought in the Crusades?'

'Yes.'

'And saw many battles I'm sure.'

'Many.'

'Such a waste of life for a pointless cause.' Jerrard took a sip of water from his flask and offered it to Nasir. 'The Crusades were nothing like as important as the fight you have here.'

'A battle without end.' The gleam to the Saracen's eyes was loaded with so much emotion and information, that Jerrard didn't need to ask him anything more on the matter. 'Robert is lucky to have you.'

Nasir bowed again, before leaning back against a tree in a companionable silence until, suddenly, he stood up straight. 'Robin is coming.'

Jerrard then saw what Nasir had merely sensed. Robert of Huntingdon; the boy turned man, his blonde hair framing his face, his expression as curious as it was cautious, had arrived with Much at his side.

'Jerrard! It *is* you!' Robin engulfed the old man in an embrace. 'This is wonderful.' He stepped back, his hands resting on his former companion's shoulders. 'Much tells me you've been working in Nottingham castle.'

'Yes, Master Robert. For your father.'

'The earl has men in Nottingham castle?' Robin's forehead creased in surprise. 'How many?'

'Just me, Master Robert. However, I fear, although I paved my way to return, it might not be safe for me to do so, thus removing your father's only honest source of information from the castle. It will depend on the success of my mission.'

'Mission?' Robin stepped back to regard his old companion closer, 'Is that why you're here?'

'It is.'

Robin's friendly expression held, but he could feel an unwanted trickle of suspicion run down his spine. 'Why would my father have a spy in the castle?'

'To look out for you, Master Robert. Why else?'

Indicating to Nasir and Much that they should take the deer to Tuck, Robin sat on the fallen tree trunk next to his guest. 'It is good to see you, Jerrard, but you must forgive me for I have learned the hard way to be wary. Since Lord Edgar played games with my family loyalty, I am slow to trust.'

'Your uncle? Hmm, yes, I would worry if you trusted anyone at all, Master Robert. You'd never have survived in Sherwood this long otherwise.' Jerrard abruptly changed the subject, 'How's your father, do you know?'

Robin's eyes dipped to the forest floor, his good cheer evaporating. 'He was well when I last saw him.'

'And when was that?'

'The same time he last saw me.' Leaving his cryptic answer hanging in the air, Robin picked up a twig and played it through his fingers. 'Much said you were being followed by the Sheriff's captain.'

'Flynn,' Jerrard's expression became more serious. 'He's been blackmailing Gisburne. I overheard.'

'Gisburne? Why?'

Jerrard lowered his voice. 'Have you heard of the Knights of the Apocalypse?'

Robin threw down the twig and looked up sharply. 'Apocalypse?'

'Master Robert?'

'I've heard that word. I was warned by Herne.' His gaze drifted into the trees. 'It felt like a danger that was far away.'

'Whatever danger they bring with them, I fear it is closing in.' Jerrard unhooked his bag from his shoulder. 'Whoever these knights are, they are clever. They live in the shadows, using rumour to their advantage. I wasn't convinced they were real, but now...' He threw his hands in the air. 'Not even the sheriff is sure of the manner of their existence however.'

'I've heard gossip of an order of noblemen that is said to influence the Pope?' Robin threw down the twig, 'One that seeks to control the Church, yes? This order seems to go hand in glove with fear of the Interdict.'

'That's them—the Order of the Holy Apocalypse.'

'*They* are the Apocalypse Herne spoke of?' Instinct sent Robin's hand to rest on Albion as he asked, 'What does this have to do with Gisburne?'

'Maybe nothing.' Jerrard sighed, 'As I said, I overheard him and Flynn talking. Flynn was extorting money from Sir Guy over a secret he's keeping from Robert de Rainault. Apparently Gisburne has a tunic hidden away in his chamber.'

'A tunic? From a uniform?'

'That was the impression I got.'

'And Guy paid up?'

'He did.' Jerrard shuffled around to face his companion. 'Now why would he do that if he didn't have something to hide?'

'And you think it's the Apocalypse colours Gisburne had hidden?'

'In truth, I don't know. But I *do* know that there's a difference in Sir Guy since he got back from France.' Jerrard grimaced. 'He has an air about him that, for all his taunting, even unsettles the sheriff.'

Robin stood up, 'I think we should join the others. They should hear about this.'

As he got to his feet, Jerrard laid a hand on Robin's shoulder. 'Some of it, yes. Some of it they must know. But there is something we need to discuss that they shouldn't be told.'

'Such as?'

Jerrard took a deep breath, 'Your father's most profound secret.'

Robin flew round, his eyes narrow, 'You know?'

'I know.'

'My father told you?' Robin's frown intensified. '*When* did he tell you?'

Jerrard let out a ragged groan as he saw the flash of distrust in Robin's eyes. 'You have little confidence in your father's word? Even though he swore otherwise, you still think he knew of Guy's patronage before you told him?'

'I...'

'It is healthy to have doubts, but I can assure you, Robert, that the earl did *not* know he'd fathered Margaret's son until you told him.'

Robin was stung by shame when he saw how his mistrust had saddened his old friend. 'I don't mean to doubt him. We have become so estranged. Not surprisingly. I'm hardly the son he hoped for.'

'Yet he is still proud of all you do and he wouldn't lie to you. I can't say he'd never hold information back from you, if he believed it was the best thing to do, but lie—no. The earl is a man of honour as well as being your father.'

Robin said nothing as the servant went on.

'After he discovered, from you, that he'd sired another, the earl came to Nottingham and told me everything. And so, from the moment Guy came home, I've been keeping an ear out for you, Master Robert, his heir, and an eye and ear on Huntingdon's unknowing pretender.'

His countenance grave, Robin gestured along the path that ultimately led to the castle. 'Does Flynn know of this too?'

'No. But what he knows, or thinks he knows, about Gisburne, was serious enough to have him follow me out of the castle into Sherwood when he realised I'd overheard their conversation.'

'We must make sure Flynn has left the forest. I don't like the idea of de Rainault's captain so close to our camp.' Robin slapped his friend on the back, 'Come on, I'd like you to meet everyone.' He smiled, 'and you must forgive me again. Thoughts of my father made me forget my manners. I haven't asked how you are.'

'Old and aching, Master Robert, but well enough. I'll be all the better however, when you and

I—*together*—have been to see your father.'

The deer Nasir had delivered to Tuck was laid out across a fallen trunk at the furthest point of the camp, ready to be skinned. As Robin and Jerrard approached, the servant clapped his hands in delight as he saw the sheriff's former chaplain bent over the beast, a sharp knife to hand.

'Good day, Brother Tuck. How fortunate for your friends that the prevailing wind will take the stench of precooked venison away from the camp.'

'Jerrard?' Tuck thrust the knife into the loose skin at the deer's neck and straightened up, wiping his hands on his apron. 'Why bless me!'

Seeing Tuck's joy, Marion turned to face the newcomer, before jumping to her feet. 'It is you! How long it's been.'

Exchanging a puzzled shrug with Little John as they sat together by the fire, Will Scarlet asked, 'Did you all go to a feast we missed? How come you know each other?'

'There weren't many feasts in Nottingham back then, Will.' Throwing her arms around their guest, Marion's smile was wide. 'Jerrard was one of the good guys. Always there with extra blankets in the winter and cooling cloths in the heat. And he used to help me with my bees when the sheriff allowed it.'

'Bees which thrive to this day, Lady Marion.' He gave a low bow. 'I've made it my business to keep an eye on your hives. Nottingham has never been the same since you left, although,' he looked proudly around him, 'thank God you did, or the people of Sherwood would be in even worse straits than they are.'

Crossing his arms over his ample belly, Tuck chuckled, 'Jerrard was a handy man to have around the chapel in the depths of winter too. Proper cold it got in there I can tell you. A man with access to hot meats and warm ale from the kitchen is a man worth his weight in gold.'

'Always thinking with your stomach even then, eh, Tuck?' John threw a lump of bread playfully at the friar.

Jerrard laughed, 'It's heartening to be remembered so fondly. The sheriff has gone through chaplains like water since then. None but you seem to have the required backbone to stay in Nottingham and deal with his unique take on prayer for long.'

'You mean you *saw* him pray?' Tuck was genuinely shocked.

'Not once. Unless you count his eager mumbling over the counting table.'

Robin turned from Tuck to Marion. 'It hadn't occurred to me that you'd know Jerrard too.'

Marion reached out a hand to Robin. 'I like that we have someone from our pasts in common.'

John offered Jerrard a flask of ale. 'Sit down, friend. You must have some stories to tell about these rogues!'

'Oh, I do.' The servant flashed a grin at Marion and Tuck, before winking at Robin. 'Especially this one. You should have seen him as a young pup, running his maid servant round in circles. Light of her life he was.'

'But for now, such stories must wait.' Robin's tone cut through the light-hearted atmosphere. 'The captain of the guard is still in the forest.'

Nasir, anticipating the order he was about to receive, got to his feet. 'He was heading as if to Lincoln. The Papplewick road.'

'Papplewick's where I told the cook I was going. Pretended I had a sick family member to go and care for.'

Robin pointed to the east. 'Will, go with Nasir. If Flynn is lost in the forest, steer him back to Nottingham. I want him safely out of here.'

'Safely? Surely an arrow in the back is the safest course for everyone long term,' Will sneered. 'Or 'ave you forgotten his attempts to catch us while Gisburne was away playing soldiers? Then there was his hand in capturing John before he married Meg!'[1]

John got to his feet. 'Yeah, and he—'

'Nothings forgotten.' Robin cut across his men, his voice brooking no argument, before he modified his tone. 'Sorry, I didn't mean to snap. For now, I have a feeling we'll be better off with him alive.'

'Why?' John's eyebrows knitted together, he'd never forgive Flynn for endangering his marriage.

'Because Flynn's blackmailing Gisburne, and—'

'He's *what?*' Will was amazed.

'Jerrard overheard them.' Robin stared into the depths of Sherwood. 'I'd like to find out what Gisburne is up to. For that, we need Flynn back in the castle making Guy's life uncomfortable enough to flush him out. With any luck Guy will flee this way, and we can ask him ourselves.'

---

1   See *To Have and to Hold*, adapted by Eliott Thorpe from a story by Barnaby Eaton-Jones.

CHAPTER 4

Marion held Robin's hand as they sat around the campfire with Much, John and Tuck, listening to tales of how Robin's mother had encouraged Jerrard to teach her son how to merge into the forest behind Huntingdon castle, making himself invisible.

While she laughed along with their friends, Marion sensed Robin was only half listening. He might have been nodding and smiling in all the right places, but his mind was elsewhere.

'I can hear Lady Mathilda now…' Jerrard was enjoying his audience's reaction to his reminiscences. 'The times she argued with his Lordship over what she encouraged young Master Robert to get up to. She was convinced that every young man needed to know every method of survival available to them in the "treacherous times we live in".'

'Sensible woman.' Marion felt Robin's hand tense in hers.

Jerrard chuckled. 'Sensible bravery. That's what she called it.'

Oblivious to Robin's unease, Much took a bite of an apple, asking as he chewed, 'Are you the one who taught Robin to shoot?'

'In time, yes, but it was his mother first off. You should have seen the pride on your leader's face when, at four years old, Lady Mathilda presented him with his first bow.'

Robin gave a drawn out sigh, 'My father was not impressed.'

'Surely he wanted you to learn the skills of a knight from an early age?' John was surprised.

'Of a knight, yes. I'd had a sword since I was three. Ridiculously heavy thing I could hardly carry.'

'The lad couldn't wield it for the life of him. Although that never prevented you trying, Master Robert.' Jerrard winked. 'Miracle you didn't take your own ear off!'

Robin snorted at the memory. 'My father was fine with that, but he hated that mother had given me a simple peasant's bow, not a fancy knight's one.'

Seeing a shadow pass over his former charge's eyes, Jerrard was worried. The rift between the father and son of Huntingdon was clearly far more entrenched than he'd feared. He had assumed it had begun once Robert had adopted the mantle of an outlaw, but now saw that it had started long ago.

How can I help them heal now, before it's too late?

'There were three of us who cared for Robert while his mother was alive, myself, Aland and Edgar.'

'Not *Lord* Edgar?' Much was shocked.

'No, lad, Master Robert's uncle never cared for anything that didn't result in furthering his own cause. *Our* Edgar was a kind soul, and an expert with the quarterstaff.'

'Ah, so he was the one who taught you?' John grinned. 'He did a fair enough job.'

'Father never did find out about that.' Robin paused, lost in memories. 'They were good people.'

'They were. I miss them.' Jerrard took another sip of ale. 'After your father sent me to Nottingham, Aland and Edgar stayed with you, Robert, of course. The Lord took them when their time was right.'

'Huntingdon was never the same.' Grateful for Marion's calm presence, Robin held her close. 'I was only eight when I lost my mother, but she'd already taught me so much. I didn't know then what path I was destined to walk, but I've often wondered if my mother did. If she sensed somehow that I'd need to know how to cope beyond the comforts of a cold castle.'

'Maybe Herne spoke to her?' Much shuffled uncomfortably. 'Maybe he saw that one day, if... if Robin of Loxley fell, then...'

Jerrard put a kind hand out to the youngest outlaw. 'While Lady Mathilda had time for the people and understood their need for forest gods, I doubt she believed in them. She was, after all, the daughter of the Earl of Chester, and lived many miles from Sherwood.'

Robin smiled at Much, showing him he didn't mind him mentioning Loxley. 'My father hardly ever spoke of my mother after she'd gone. Only once did he open up. When I was sixteen. He'd caught me poaching pheasants for the cook and flew into one of his rages. I raged back and somehow we ended up talking about mother, about how they'd met... She didn't sound like someone who'd talk to spirits in the forest, more someone who'd challenge kings.'[2]

Jerrard laughed. 'Indeed she would. And did! Her father despaired of her.'

Marion's eyes shone with amusement. 'I can see where you get it from, Robin.'

---

2   See *Mathilda's Legacy*, written by Jennifer Ash.

Abruptly serious, Jerrard shook his head, 'If you'd told me then that I'd end up working for the Sheriff of Nottingham, for the sake of appearances at least, I'd have thought you a fool, and yet now… Perhaps it was meant to be.' The old man lapsed into silence before he finally said, 'Do you remember the first time you met de Rainault, Robert?'

'I was about seven, I think. He came to Huntingdon with Abbot Hugo, I don't recall why.'

'Ah, so he did. Although Hugo was just a humble prior with intentions of grandeur back then. But no, that was the second time. The first time was in Nottingham castle when you were nowt but three years old.'

'I don't remember that.' Robin took the ale pouch from John. 'Why was I there?'

'Your parents were travelling back from York to Huntingdon and had stopped at Nottingham for a night's rest.' Jerrard tugged at his beard as he thought. 'The reason for the trip eludes my memory, but I shall never forget the day. De Rainault hadn't held the position long, a year, maybe two. He was young and, if possible, even more ambitious than he is now. He was determined to wipe away any sign of the previous sheriff's time in office.'

'God help us!' Tuck crossed himself.

'It was long before you were Hugo's ward, Lady Marion, and before you came to be his chaplain Tuck. You, Master Robert, were lined up with your mother and her maids to be introduced to the sheriff, before being shown your quarters.'

'While my father stayed and ate with the sheriff. I suppose.'

The sarcastic lilt to Robin's voice saddened Jerrard. 'That is his job, Robert. To talk, to listen, and to protect the land on behalf of the king if he needs to. This means he has to spend time with a lot of people he cannot abide.'

'You know the earl doesn't like the sheriff, Robin.' Marion coaxed, 'I'm sure he would far rather have spent the night with his family.'

'Indeed he would, my Lady.' Jerrard watched Robin out of the corner of his eye as he continued. 'His Lordship often complained of the colossal waste of time the obligation of his position caused; time he could spend with his wife and son.'

'Did he?'

'You are surprised?' Jerrard levelled his gaze on Robin. 'Yet you don't doubt his love for you, surely? Have I, or have I not, been positioned in Nottingham castle to watch over the sheriff, with particular intent on his plans for you and your friends?'

Even the flicker of the campfire seemed to hold its breath in curiosity as Robin asked, 'So what happened between me and the sheriff when I was three?'

Jerrard chuckled, 'De Rainault was showing off. As you were introduced, you stepped forward and bowed, just as your father had taught you. Rather than bowing back, the sheriff threw you a silver mark to catch—but you hadn't been expecting it, and missed. I can't recall exactly what your father said, but I do remember he was not impressed that you'd been treated as if you were a passing minstrel, paid to perform, rather than the heir of the most important earldom in England. Your mother stepped in and managed to gloss over the slight by making it into a game. She told you the sheriff was playing catch and that you should throw the coin back, which you did. Unfortunately—or fortunately, to hear Lady Mathilda talk of it later—you were not practised in throwing either. You hurled that mark so fast and so high, that it hit de Rainault in the face, giving him a black eye.'

John and Much gave Robin a round of applause.

'I don't remember that at all.'

Tuck grinned. 'Just shows that the good Lord has a healthy sense of humour.'

Marion smiled, 'I bet de Rainault remembers though, Robin.'

'No wonder he doesn't like me very much.'

'Who doesn't like you very much?' Will arrived back at the camp with Nasir at his side. 'Your father?'

'The sheriff.' Robin stood up as his friends arrived, 'Flynn?'

'On the road to the castle.' Will crouched by the fire. 'Running at full pelt. It seems something scared him half to death in the forest.'

Much nudged his friend's shoulder. 'Was it you what frightened him, Will?'

'Nah.' Scarlet took some ale from Tuck, 'it was that scary Saracen I hang about with.'

Nasir bowed, a faint smile playing around his lips as he sheathed the two swords he held before him.

CHAPTER 5

The sound of Tuck and John skinning the deer, while Much set up a spit to roast it on, floated across the camp as Jerrard and Robin walked a little way into the forest.

'It was good to talk about your mother again.' Jerrard regarded Robin shrewdly. Now they were alone, he wasn't sure how to begin the conversation they needed to have.

'Sometimes her memory is so clear, then other times…,' Robin ran a hand though his hair, 'It's as if she was just a dream.'

'As it always is when we lose someone we love.'

'I was barely a child.'

'She was your mother, and you loved her. Just as your father did.' Jerrard gestured to a clear patch of ground and sat down. 'Or should I say, still does.'

Robin opened his mouth to speak, but Jerrard stopped him.

'I know you see your father as hard and inflexible, but you are not a fool, Robert. You know his position demands that he must conceal his feelings least they be seen as weakness by his enemies.'

'Enemies?' Robin's head shot up. 'He is threatened?'

'Ah…' Jerrard felt an easing of the tension in his shoulders. 'So you do care for him?'

'Of course I care. He's my father. But he's so… so…'

'So like his son?' Jerrard opened his scrip and broke a piece of bread in half, passing some to Robin. 'You inherited your drive to do good, your passion to help, and your survival instincts from your mother. But those alone are not enough to keep Herne's Son alive. You need to make cold hard decisions. You have to think quickly. And you, as Robin Hood, are the one who, when the time comes, makes the decisions that are the difference between life and death. Remind you of anyone?'

Unable to argue with what he was hearing, Robin took a mouthful of bread, wondering if he should tell Jerrard he'd been seeing his mother in his dreams.

'The Earl of Huntingdon, like your grandfather before him, has spent his whole life having to be seen to be in control. Immovable, austere, commanding. Not all of it's an act—but most of it is.'

Robin snorted. 'He's convincing.'

'Yes he is.' Jerrard gave a half smile. 'And if your two superiors in England were King John and the Archbishop of Canterbury—who is little more than the Pope's puppet, anyway—wouldn't *you* need to act thus? And isn't is possible that you'd become so used to behaving that way, that unbending to show any sort of positive emotion would become difficult? That however much you wanted to fling your arms around your son, you'd feel unable to do so?'

Robin brushed some breadcrumbs from his hands. He could hear Tuck in the background bickering with John and Will about how to get the deer on the spit; telling them that if they didn't get on with it there would be no venison this side of Christmas.

'You asked when I last saw the earl.' Robin peered at Jerrard through his fringe. 'But you already know.'

'Not if you've seen him since you travelled to Huntingdon after your encounter with Morgwyn of Ravenscar.'[3]

---

3   See *The Power of Three* by Jennifer Ash.

'I haven't.'

'That was several months ago.' Jerrard found himself adopting a tone he hadn't used since cajoling Robert into doing something he didn't want to do when he was a boy. 'Your father is older than I am, and I am no youngster.'

'Guilt.' The word shot out of Robin's mouth like an arrow from a bow.

Startled, Jerrard protested, 'I didn't mean to make you feel guilty, Master Robert, I...'

Robin brushed the notion away. 'Forgive me, no, I meant, guilt is what's stopped me going back to see him.' The outlaw shuffled forward, desperately hoping his childhood companion would understand. 'He *is* an old man. I know that. And I know what it will mean for him, for me, and for Huntingdon when his time comes.'

Jerrard bit his tongue, leaving space for Robin, hoping he'd continue.

'I treated my father badly. I didn't mean to—I never do mean to. Just as I'm sure he never means to sound disappointed in me, and yet...'

'Your father told me about what happened when Morgwyn bewitched you. You were not yourself.'

'Ah, but I was.' Robin drew his dagger and stabbed it into the earth before him in frustration.

43

'At least, I suspect I was. I suspect I was the man I would have been if I had never come to the forest.'

'Go on.'

'I was so sure he already knew that Guy was his son. Even before Morgwyn filled my blood with her poisoned ink, I'd assumed he'd always known my life was a lie. That I wasn't really his first born, and that all that training to mould me into the perfect heir could have been inflicted on another if not for a twist of fate.'

'The spell Morgwyn cast enhanced your fears. It took your worst thoughts, exaggerated them and turned them against you.' Jerrard paused. 'At least, that's how your father tells it.'

'And he was right. I questioned everything. Even...' he held his hands up indicating the trees that towered above them, protecting them from the heat of the approaching midday sun, '...even if I should stay here. Whether I had the right to be Herne's Son.'

'And what did you do then? Once the spell had been broken and your outlaw friends celebrated your safe return to them?'

'I went to Huntingdon.' Robin exhaled a puff of air, 'Marion persuaded me to go, to apologise to my father. I hurt him. Physically and emotionally.'

'And so you went home.'

'To say sorry.' Robin shrugged, 'I thought maybe we could talk, but it became an argument. Only a day or so before, he'd told me I was always welcome at Huntingdon; that I must never deny my destiny, or use Huntingdon to hide from it. Even though I'd been so cruel to him, he'd been kind. But once I got to Huntingdon, risking my life to break into the castle, hiding from his guards, just so I could visit him…'

As Robin's words petered off, Jerrard took over, his words gentle. 'When he was here, with you in Sherwood, he was your father. When he is within the castle, he is the Earl of Huntingdon. Just as you are Robin of Sherwood. Do you understand?'

'Unfortunately, I do.'

'I knew you would,' Jerrard nodded fervently, 'which is why I'm here. Time is running out, Master Robert. I can feel it. When I overheard Flynn and Gisburne a sense of foreboding overcame me like I've never known before. I swear I could hear a voice in my head that was not my own—and yet it *was* my own. It urged me to find you and warn you.'

'Warn me that one high ranking solider is blackmailing another, and that that blackmail might have something to do with an order of knights, that may or may not exist?'

45

Tempted to tell Robin he'd sounded just like his father, but resisting the urge, Jerrard said, '*If* the Knights of the Apocalypse are real, and *if* Gisburne is one of them, what if they find out that he has a tenuous entitlement to one of the most important Earldoms in England?'

'How would they find out, though?' Robin frowned. 'Guy doesn't even know.'

'Morgwyn of Ravenscar found out. She isn't the only sorcerer in the land. What if the order uses magic? There seems something unearthly about the whispers that surround them. What if they target your father? Not an improbable idea as he holds a fine earldom. The consequences…'

'Could be disastrous for my father. For England.' Robin grimaced. 'If Guy was the earl then…'

Jerrard was solemn. 'This country has enough cruel men ruling it. Huntingdon has always been a valuable exception. The earldom requires an even-handed man in charge.'

'I can't.' Robin closed his eyes to hide the guilt he feared might show in them. 'I made a pledge to Herne, to my friends, to Sherwood.'

'And I'm not asking you to break it. I'm asking you to come with me to the earl, to tell him of my concerns before it's too late.'

'Um…' Robin was thoughtful. 'These concerns sparked by an overheard conversation, they are just theories. You have no proof that Guy is involved with the knights.'

'None at all. My fears are based on an instinct alone.'

'I can't leave Sherwood unprotected over a gut feeling.'

Jerrard's head tilted to one side as he asked, 'But when Herne speaks to you, isn't that all riddles and instinct and gut feelings?'

Robin's forehead creased, 'Who told you about Herne's riddles?'

'Your father.' Jerrard smiled, 'He respects your instincts. He also respects mine. I am asking you, Master Robert, for old times' sake, to trust them too. If we go and tell him of my fears over Guy, then perhaps you can help the earl find a way to choose a worthy successor. Someone who'd have your blessing in the role. It would free you from the guilt of not being the heir he expected you to be, and your father can die at peace, knowing Huntingdon is in good hands.'

Lapsing into silence again, Robin inhaled the first scents of cooking meat. He could imagine Much rotating the spit, bemoaning that it was always him that ended up turning the handle for hours at a time. A smile briefly appeared on his face as he thought how – when the time finally came for eating the result – Much would say what he always said, "t'was worth all that spitting."

He wondered what Marion was doing. He'd have liked to talk to her, but Robin was sure she'd have packed him off to Huntingdon already.

She doesn't know about Guy.

Robin chewed another mouthful of bread as he reflected that, in fact, Marion did know. Morgwyn had told her, but she had chosen not to believe it. Had thought it part of the witches evil to tear the outlaws apart.

I should have told her it was true.

Finishing his bread, Jerrard got to his feet. 'If you won't come to Huntingdon, then I must go alone. I swore to tell your father of any danger to you, to Huntingdon and to the Crown. Gisburne's potential involvement with the knights involves all three of those things.'

Robin stayed where he was; thinking over all Jerrard had told him. 'And Gisburne, whether the knights are involved or not, is being blackmailed. That means Guy has done something that he doesn't want the Sheriff to know about.'

'Which means it's probably dangerous,' Jerrard agreed, 'and so the Earl should know.'

'It's a long walk.' Robin's conscience nudged at him. 'You should at least stay for some food before you go.'

Jerrard gestured in the direction of the camp. 'I have heard Tuck is a good cook.'

'He is. We are lucky to have him.'

'Don't the others cook?'

'Sometimes.' Robin smiled despite himself, 'But not John. Once was enough.'

They lapsed into silence, until Jerrard asked, 'Why do you think that, even before you knew of your connection to him, you've never killed Guy, nor allowed your men to finish him off?'

'He's useful alive.' Robin's answer was quick. His eyes lifted to Jerrard, challenging him to disagree. But the old man did just that.

'He is *not* useful. The Sheriff keeps him because he is a convenient stooge to his wit. He likes an audience, does de Rainault. Over the years Guy has become the sheriff's court jester, his pet even. They operate apart yet work well together. Their mutual hate sparks productivity. Their oppression of the people happens because they are a team; albeit one spurred on by greed and ambition. If you were to take Guy away, you'd almost certainly have a weaker sheriff.

'He would be replaced by another though, Jerrard. We might get an efficient deputy sheriff. That would not be good for the people.'

'Or it might be better for them to have someone who might dare to disagree with the sheriff.'

'He and Guy disagree all the time!'

'No, they argue all the time. It's not the same thing.'

'Perhaps.' Robin pulled Albion from its sheath, moving the sword so the sun reflected off the bright sharp blade.

Jerrard sat back down. 'That sword, it is as much as symbol for good as you are. It only kills those you have no choice but to slay. Am I right?'

'Yes.'

'But you control the sword, Master Robert. You decide who lives and dies with it. That's important.'

Robin kept his eyes on Albion, 'Sometimes I make the wrong choices.'

'Sometimes we all do,' Jerrard nodded. 'I know the real reason why you've never killed Sir Guy, Master Robert. I know why.'

CHAPTER 6

Robin could almost hear the fire in the grate and smell the wood smoke as it funnelled upwards, blackening the inside of vast chimney of Huntingdon's great hall.

It had been over twenty years since he'd thought of Edwin. With his mind a turmoil of regrets concerning his father, Robin closed his eyes and let Jerrard's words washed over him.

Edwin's hair had been blonde like his own. Everyone had joked that they were like brothers. But Robert's mother had been about to give him a real brother. 'Or sister!' Robin was warmed by the memory. Suddenly he could see his mother, her belly swollen beneath her skirts, regarding his father with definite but smiling clarity, reminding him that there was more than one gender in the world.

The earl had been insistent, however. Persistent in his belief that she would bear him another boy. A second son to firmly tie the earldom to his family.

Another memory collided with the first, as Robin, eight yours old, his mother gone, stood with Jerrard, lost and confused, as his father sat and cried.

'Perhaps, if it had been a girl… she'd wanted a girl… but I…'

Robin shook himself.

Edwin. My first friend.

He'd been the son of local knight who'd fallen in a battle long forgotten. And then, only two winters later, Edwin's mother had succumbed to a fever and joined her husband in the cold crypt of Lincoln cathedral. People had whispered that grief had weakened her to the ravages of the malady that had taken her, and that she'd had no heart left in her to fight it.

Edwin had been a head taller than Robin, stockier and stronger. A fact he was extremely proud of. They'd been inseparable from the age of seven. Mathilda, taking pity upon the boy who'd lost both mother and father so young, had welcomed Edwin into the family; treating him like a son.

It had seemed natural then, a year later, when his mother had gone into labour, for the earl to ask his brother, Lord Edgar, to take Robert and Edwin away from Huntingdon until the birth was over.

That must have been the third time I met the sheriff. I wonder if he remembers?

Robin felt the hairs stand up on the back of his neck as he began to recall that particular trip to Nottingham castle...

'Robert, my boy, come up here. Come on.'

Lord Edgar tapped the edge of the high table, where he was sat with the Sheriff. 'You're the heir to Huntingdon. You should not be sat with the ordinary *guests.' Edgar swung round, savouring the sight of the Sheriff wrestling with his facial expression as he considered the prospect of being in close proximity to children. 'Don't you agree, de Rainault? A future heir to the most important earldom in England should not eat with servants.'*

'Forgive me, Lord Edgar, you are quite right.' De Rainault shooed the nearest servant into action, 'Make a place for the boy, woman. It should have been done before!'

Robert glanced at Jerrard, who confirmed that position really was being granted to sit at the most important table in the castle. 'If your uncle and the sheriff wish it, then you must go.'

Edwin clapped his hands in glee, his chest puffed out with the honour of it, pompous in his keenness to get to the superior fare on offer. 'Come on Robert, let's go.'

'Sorry Edwin,' Jerrard placed a hand on the lad's shoulder, his voice kind. 'It's just the earl's heir who is requested. We must stay here.'

Stricken, his young face scarlet with embarrassment at both his assumption and the personal slight to his own importance, Edwin had slunk back to his chair, not looking at his friend.

'I'd rather stay here with you,' Robert had muttered as he stood up to obey his uncle. 'I'll bring you some food back.'

Pretending indifference, Edwin turned away. 'I didn't want to go anyway.'

Feeling awkward, and resentful towards his uncle for putting him in this position, Robert walked up to the high table. He could feel the sheriff's toad-like eyes on him; accessing and somehow accusing him of something so far undone.

'May I present Robert of Huntingdon, my Lord de Rainault?'

'We have met before.'

Robert bowed as he was instructed while speaking the lines his father would expect him to say. 'I'm honoured to be granted a seat at your table, my Lord.'

'Your uncle speaks well of you.'

'Does he, my Lord?' The surprise in his voice made the sheriff laugh and Lord Edgar's distinctive lopsided smile falter.

'You're my nephew, Robert. Would you expect me to speak otherwise?'

'No, my Lord, I simply meant that...'

'Your father would not be pleased to know you'd assumed so much. Now, sit quietly and eat your meat, else I report to the earl that you aren't worthy of the high office to which an accident of birth has given you.'

Robert felt the heat of the sheriff's pleasure as Lord Edgar told him off in front of everyone. He wanted to look at Edwin. To exchange an acknowledgement of fellowship, but something stopped him. What if Edwin is glad I was told off?

The unjust nature of his chastisement niggled at Robert all through the long drawn out meal. He tried to be a dutiful nephew, to laugh at his uncle's jokes and pretend to be amused by the sheriff's cruel humour, but they made him feel uncomfortable, and sometimes a bit sick.

Why is it alright to laugh at the plight of the poor or take joy in their suffering?

It was a relief when Jerrard, with a courteous bow to both Lord Edgar and the sheriff, came to collect him from high table to go to his bed chamber. Robert scrabbled down from the high wooden chair, with far more speed that he'd climbed upon it. Although as they got closer to the bedroom, he felt a fresh sense of unease creep over him.

What if Edwin isn't talking to me? It isn't my fault I had to leave him to eat alone. *'Is Edwin angry with me, Jerrard?'*

'His pride was hurt, but I doubt he's angry with you.' Jerrard's reply lacked some of its usual certainty, as he climbed the stairs two paces behind his young master.

'Is he already abed?'

'I believe so, Master Robert.' Jerrard shifted uneasily. *'The sheriff granted you separate chambers.'*

'But we were to share. It was going to be an adventure.' Robert stopped walking, a sensation of disquiet making the hairs on his neck stand up. *'Edwin hasn't been put with the servants, has he? He's my friend. The same as me.'*

'With respect, Master Robert, while he is your friend, he is not the same as you. He is not your equal. He is the son of a knight. His father was wealthy once, but his mother spent so much on his tomb that there was little left and… in short, Master Robert, young Master Edwin will not have the future he was expecting to

have. A title yes, but depleted lands, which, by the time he is of age, may well have disappeared.'

'Disappeared? How?'

'Until he is of age, his estate is in your uncle's control, and Lord Edgar is...' Jerrard paused, uncertain how to continue. 'Not as careful as your father.'

'Well that shall not be!' Robert's voice rose, his outcry echoing along the stone corridor and bouncing off the stairs. 'I shall give him land. I shall make sure Edwin has all he needs when he comes to age. When I'm earl no one will go without if I can help it.'

Jerrard ruffled the boy's hair affectionately. 'You are your mother's son for sure.'

Marion wiped a stray blonde hair from Robin's eyes as they sat alone beneath the trees. She could hear Jerrard and Tuck nearby, happily reminiscing about their mutual time in the castle. The aroma of cooking venison wafting across the forest was making her mouth water, but she wasn't sure Robin would have much appetite when the meat was finally cooked.

'Did you tell Edwin the next morning that you'd make sure he had land when he was older?'

'It didn't work out like that.' Robin wrapped an arm around her shoulder. 'You remember that Jerrard said I'd thrown a mark at the sheriff and given him a black eye?'

'By accident when you were three!'

'Yes. I don't remember doing that, and I didn't have any idea when I was eight either. Now Jerrard has told me about it, what happened with Edwin makes more sense.'

'How do you mean? What did happen?'

'The following morning I discovered that Edwin hadn't been forced to sleep with the servants. In fact, with hindsight, I don't think he'd slept at all. Not that he was suffering from lack of sleep. He was elated.'

Marion was surprised. 'I thought you were going to say he was sulking over the night before.'

'I'd expected him to be cross with me. I hadn't slept much myself. I rehearsed over and over what I'd say, about how I couldn't help it if my uncle made me sit with him, and that when I was earl, he'd always be welcome at the top table. I was going to tell him he'd have lands of his own. I'd wanted it to sound right so I didn't patronise him, but... well, that conversation never happened.

'Edwin came running up to me as Jerrard and I entered the hall for breakfast. He was so proud as he led the way to the top table, showing me that we were both to sit with the sheriff this time. And so we did.'

'You shared breakfast with the Sheriff of Nottingham?' Marion laughed, 'Now that's one for the balladeers.'

Robin smiled, 'Edwin sat between me and de Rainault. I remember thinking that my father would not have liked that I wasn't sat next to the sheriff, but he wasn't there, and I didn't care about the rights and wrong of where a nobleman should sit. I was just glad my friend was happy again.'

'Another reason why I love you.' Marion rested her head on Robin's shoulder as she listened to his story.

'Everything was good. We laughed together about how we'd rule the kingdom one day. The sheriff even joined in, encouraging us with sycophantic comments.

'The food was already there, on the table when I arrived. "The sheriff and I have arranged a breakfast feast fit for an earl". That's what Edwin said.'

Marion's eyes narrowed. 'He'd done something to your food?'

'He thought he had, but Robert de Rainault can't have taken kindly to having to accommodate children. Especially me—a child who outranked him, and who, I now know, had already embarrassed him in front of the Earl of Huntingdon. I will never know for sure, but I assume he made the switch while Edwin was collecting me so excitedly from the stairwell. The platters looked the same.

'Edwin plunged a knife into his leg of chicken, ready to pick it up and eat,' Robin gagged at the memory, 'but blood went everywhere. It sprayed out like a fountain all over his face, his tunic, and, more to the point, all over sheriff.'

'Oh my goodness!'

'They must have made a split in the cooked chicken, carved it out and filled it with blood from some of the fresh meat in the kitchen.'

Marion scowled, 'That would take time to set up. Edwin was set on embarrassing you.'

'He was eight and in a castle he didn't know. It has to have been the sheriff who set up the trick, or at least, had it set up for him. De Rainault getting sprayed too was just a happy accident with hindsight.' Robin grunted, 'To add to the merriment, my uncle chose just that moment to walk in.'

'What did Edwin do?'

'He leapt to his feet and began to berate me. Screaming of how I'd humiliated him and disgraced myself before the most honourable sheriff.' Robin's voice became barely a whisper, as if even now, he struggled to understand why his friend would betray him so.

'I can guess the rest.' Marion lifted her head off his shoulder and held his eyes with her own. 'Lord Edgar was furious, the sheriff backed up Edwin and you took the blame for a trick you never played.'

'I was sent back to Huntingdon in disgrace. Edwin hardly looked at me all the way home and he spoke not one word. I knew he was terrified I'd tell my father the truth about his hand in the sabotage of the food.'

'Did you?'

'No. I decided to take the blame. I had everything and Edwin was destined for a far more frugal life.' Robin ran a hand through his hair. 'My father was ruthless in his punishment. I only learnt the day after, my limbs still sore from my beating, that he was a man crippled by grief.'

'Your mother?'

'My brother had been born the night before, but she had not survived his journey into the world. And he didn't last long either,' Robin groaned, 'and then, the first thing his surviving son did was confess to soaking the Sheriff of Nottingham in chicken's blood.'

Marion winced at the scene Robin had painted. She could picture him clearly. Eight years old, his heart broken for the loss of his mother and hurting from the betrayal of his only friend, being punished by a grief ravaged father.

'Edwin was like a brother to you.'

Robin's pulse quickened at her observation. 'Jerrard reminded me of this incident because of Gisburne. He said, thinking of Edwin then, of how I'd taken his guilt as my own, would remind me of why I've never killed Guy. Of why I've always shown him mercy.'

'But Gisburne isn't like a brother to you he's always stood against us.'

'He has.' Robin swallowed carefully, 'and if Jerrard's fears are confirmed, he is going to again— and he won't be alone.'

'Robin?'

'Come on, we need to talk with the others.'

CHAPTER 7

'These Holy knights, if they're in France, why should we worry?' Will wiped droplets of venison grease from his chin with the back of his hand. 'Surely, if Gisburne has joined them, that means he'll be going back there.'

'And good riddance.' John added as he took a swig of ale.

'It's not that simple, Will.' Robin stared into the flames of the campfire.

'Of course it ain't. Never is.' Will grumbled as he chewed his way through a lump of meat.

Jerrard watched the Hooded Man's outlaws as they looked to their leader; they were clearly waiting for him to speak, to guide them. He'd heard so much about Robert's followers over the years. A constant stream of negativity from the sheriff and

Gisburne—in stark contrast to the good word from the folk of the forest. He'd heard how brave they were; that they were heroes who'd never stop fighting in the face of tyranny. Yet, as he sat with them now, Jerrard didn't see one woman and six men trying to be heroic; he saw a group of ordinary people, battle hardened by the life they led.

That's Guy's mistake. He craves acceptance and praise for everything he does. He needs to be seen to be powerful. It hasn't occurred to him that, compared to most, he already is.

The old man's gaze switched to Marion. Despite the passage of years since she'd been a young ward determined to escape the castle, she'd hardly changed. However, there was a different type of determination about her now; and a sadness too. A sense that she held with her the knowledge that the life they lived could end tomorrow.

Robin finally broke his silence. 'Herne told me to be aware of the Apocalypse after your wedding, John. I didn't understand what he meant at the time; didn't connect it with the rumours from the Church about the Interdict.'

Tuck gave a sudden loud belch, making everyone look in his direction.

Much giggled, 'Tuck!'

'Oh, pardon me!' His ruddy cheeks flushed as he displayed his approval of his own cooking. 'Robin, the Pope is greedy. He'll do anything to squeeze more money out the churches.'

'How does closing them earn 'im money though?' Much was confused.

'Because he can demand money for the privilege of them being reopened,' explained Tuck, 'along with extracting a promise from King John that he won't be a naughty boy again, and see his churches operate properly. In other words, as Pope Innocent decides they should be run. By his law, rather than God's Holy Law—although he seems to change his mind on what that actually means on an almost weekly basis.'

'Isn't the Church run properly now then?' Much asked as he soaked up some venison grease with a portion of bread.

'Depends who's asking,' Tuck shrugged.

Marion turned to Jerrard. 'This blackmail exchange you overheard between Flynn and Gisburne. You are convinced it was about *these* knights?'

'I am. Every instinct in me tells me so, but that doesn't change the fact that I only overheard them. I have no proof. I'm just a servant. My word in Nottingham counts for very little.'

'We need to be sure.' Robin was thoughtful. 'Do you think if you told the sheriff about what you'd overheard, he'd believe you?'

'Without proof, no.' Jerrard shook his head. 'I've been, as far as he is concerned, loyal to him for many years. I have no reason to bring him a false tale. But without evidence I doubt he'd take me seriously. He would think it scurrilous gossip.'

'Although…' Marion mused, 'if you were to sow the seeds of doubt in the sheriff's mind, even if he publicly didn't believe what you told him, you might make him suspicious enough to order someone to search Gisburne's chamber.'

'Indeed he might.' Jerrard swivelled around so he was looking straight at Robin. 'Marion's right. Even if he dismissed what I told him out of hand, I'd bet he'd relish using it as an excuse to embarrass Sir Guy.'

'You're right.' A smile spread over Robin's face. Something in him was as convinced that they needed to know about Gisburne's involvement—or not—with the knights as Jerrard was that he needed to see his father. 'De Rainault would never pass up an opportunity to humiliate Gisburne.'

'Why didn't you hunt for this tunic at the time?' Will asked.

'Gisburne was in his chamber and I had other priorities.'

'More important than dropping Gisburne in it with the sheriff?' Will was incredulous.

Jerrard's voice was calm and certain as he replied. 'Yes. Even more important than that.'

'What's more important than...?' John found his words cut short as Robin got to his feet.

'Jerrard doesn't work for the sheriff, he works for my father. It is his duty to report anything that happens in Nottingham to him first.'

Will stared at Jerrard with distaste, spitting out his venison as if it tasted bitter. 'A spy?'

Nasir broke his habitual silence, sparing Jerrard the need to justify himself. 'Some spies work *for* us. Some against.'

Marion leaned forward, and kissed Jerrard's cheek, 'You have been keeping an eye on Robin for the earl from Nottingham haven't you?'

'I have, my Lady.' Blushing at her kiss, Jerrard was glad of her understanding. 'But not just that. The earl has never trusted de Rainault. It suits him and the king to have the sheriff discreetly observed.'

Robin added, 'Jerrard was on his way to my father to tell him of his fears about Gisburne and his possible connection to these Knights of the Apocalypse when he realised Flynn was following him. If Gisburne really is one of them—the right-hand to the Sheriff of Nottingham—then my father needs to know so he can inform King John.'

Pressing his hands to the ground, Jerrard slowly pushed himself upright. 'Which is why, my friends, I must leave you. It's a long walk to Huntingdon, and I am not as young as I was.'

'But it's almost nightfall,' Marion frowned, 'surely you won't leave until tomorrow?'

Robin threw a log onto the fire. 'I don't think you should go to Huntingdon. At least, not yet.'

'But, Master Robert,' Jerrard implored, 'I have a duty.'

'You do, but if you'd gone into the chamber and got the tunic… Will was right.'

'I was?' Scarlet spluttered some breadcrumbs down his front in surprise.

Marion protested, 'But Jerrard explained, Robin. Gisburne was in there. He could hardly walk in and ask to poke around.'

'I know. And even if you had been able to Jerrard, I imagine Guy was in a foul mood and would have chucked you out, or worse.' Robin took the old man's elbow and led him back to the fire. 'My father is no more likely to believe you without proof than the sheriff is.'

Jerrard was offended. 'He trusts my word, Master Robert.'

'I don't doubt it.' Robin squeezed the old man's arm as if to reassure him of his trust. 'But if you could *show* my father the tunic you spoke of. If he saw it... and could prove it was connected to Gisburne, he could show the king... King John would *definitely* want proof.'

'Robin,' Marion exchanged glances with Little John, 'we can't just nip into the castle and fetch it.'

'It's probably not even there anymore,' John agreed. 'Gisburne's not that big a fool. If this Flynn has already seen it, he'd have got rid of it surely.'

'I don't think so,' said Robin, scratching his head, 'not if he thinks it will bring him the success and influence he has always craved.'

'You're right, Master Robert. He'd keep it, but hide it somewhere else, somewhere better.'

'Where?' Nasir pulled a sword from its holder, examining it for potential imperfections in the fire light.

'Not in his chamber.' Jerrard's forehead furrowed as he thought. 'But there are hundreds of other places in the castle where things can be hidden away.'

'Aye, there are,' Tuck nodded. 'The chapel, the outhouses, in the kitchens even.'

'I used to hide things in an old beehive.' Marion smiled at the memory. 'Do you remember, Tuck?'

'So you did, Little Flower.'

'Didn't the bees mind, Marion?' Much asked as he pinched the last piece of venison from the platter.

'It wasn't in use. Just in the store room I shared with the gardeners. No one else went there, and the sheriff's hardly an outside person, so was unlikely to go prying.'

'Would Gisburne know of it, though?'

Marion pulled a face. 'Probably not.'

'This ain't getting us anywhere.' Will cut some more meat off the spit. 'You can't expect us to go into Nottingham to hunt for something that might not even be there, and then tell us we have to hunt the whole castle.'

'I'm not expecting any of us to, Will.' Robin turned to Jerrard. 'But *you* could.'

Jerrard sighed. 'It's possible my absence hasn't been reported by Flynn to the sheriff, but I still can't go back.'

'Why not?' Will scowled, unhappy at the idea of Jerrard being a spy, whether he was on their side or not.

'I told you. I have business with the Earl of Huntingdon.' He fixed his attention on Robin, 'There are other things that he and I need to discuss. Matters which can't be put off much longer.'

'What things?' Will muttered to John, who simply raised his eyebrows and shrugged his shoulders.

Robin leaned toward Jerrard, his manner beseeching. 'But you need only be gone a few hours. A day at most. One more day won't make much difference to my father, will it?'

Jerrard could feel the press of time tingle in his palms. 'Alright, Master Robert, I'll go back to the castle at first light.'

'Thank you.'

'But *only* if you agree to accompany me to Huntingdon to talk to your father afterwards.'

CHAPTER 8

'Come on, Tuck! You can do better than that.' John
paced around his friend, allowing him to recover
his breath after whacking him on the back with his
quarterstaff.

'Lucky swipe, that's all that was, John Little.'
Tuck circled his friend, his staff held before him.
'You won't be that lucky twice.'

As the other outlaws cheered encouragement,
Robin watched the fight. It was a plaything, an act,
but such games were vital to keep his men sharp. He
had a creeping feeling that they were going to need
to use every skill they had soon.

Apocalypse.

It was a word from stories, from fables of doom.
Suddenly Robin found himself remembering how
the Bishop of Lincoln had once scared him with

tales of the destruction of the world on a visit to Huntingdon. A memory, long forgotten, of his mother being rather curt with their visitor for filling their six-year-old's head with devilish stories made him smile—but the smile didn't last long.

What am I supposed to do? How can I fight the end of the world? It's ridiculous.

Robin knew that Herne would not have used the word "Apocalypse" after John's wedding without good reason. And now, Jerrard had come with the same word on his lips, connecting it—albeit loosely—with his father and the fate of Huntingdon.

The thwack of wood on wood echoed through the clearing, bringing Robin back to the fight before him.

'Go on, Tuck!' Will shouted from the sidelines. 'Cut that oaf down to size.'

'Yeah,' John taunted, 'come on Tuck, cut me down to size.'

The fight began again, more serious now. Robin watched his friends size each other up; admiring the skill on both sides as each gave as good as he got. For all his girth, Tuck remained light on his feet, and although he puffed and panted far more than John, he never missed his mark. Little John, his eyes focused, his arms moving so fast, they were a blur, danced from foot to foot, using his height to balance him against the weight Tuck put behind every blow.

Marion came to Robin's side as they watched. 'If we don't call it a draw soon, they'll be too exhausted to fight it they need to.'

'They have to practice.'

She noticed the absorbed expression on Robin's face. 'You think we're going to fight soon, don't you?'

'I suspect so. Something isn't right. I don't know.' Robin turned to her with a shrug.

'The Knights of the Apocalypse?'

Robin didn't answer. Hooking his bow over his shoulder, he gave her a tender kiss. 'I must go to Herne.'

Jerrard studied the spider's web that hung off the tapestry next to his cot. It was the same one he'd seen under construction before he'd left the castle. The light of his candle reflected through it, making the silky strains glisten and shine He couldn't help but admire the hard work that must have gone into its creation.

No one had challenged Jerrard as he'd walked into the castle. He'd taken the precaution of going straight to the cook, explaining that his mission to Papplewick had come too late and his kin was beyond human help. The cook had mumbled condolences, without pausing in his creation of a mountain of pie pastry.

So far Jerrard hadn't encountered either Flynn or Gisburne. He hoped he wouldn't have to. Slipping his scrip back under his cot, he knew he couldn't linger where he was. At this time of day he would normally have been checking on the sheriff's clerks, making sure they had food and drink, that their bookkeeping was up to date and that their candles hadn't run down to the point that work became impossible.

De Rainault, if his routine hadn't been disturbed by any guests or matters of state, would be in his private study grumbling his way through the paperwork that went hand-in-jewelled-glove with being a shire reeve.

With a heavy grunt, Jerrard got to his feet, hoping that the sheriff wouldn't throw him in the dungeon for announcing his news. But forcing Master Robert to engage with his father might just make it all worth it.

'I swear he gets more useless by the day!' De Rainault slammed his ledger down on the table as Flynn imparted the news that Gisburne wasn't in the castle. 'Does he expect me to run my own errands!? How am I supposed to run Nottinghamshire without an effective deputy?'

'Anything I can help with, my Lord?' Flynn tried to hide the smirk that he could feel growing on his face.

'Yes. You can get some of Gisburne's men's off their backsides and send them out to Newark. The gaol needs emptying and the prisoners bringing here for trial. You'll need to organise a prison wagon.'

'Yes, my Lord Sheriff.' Flynn gave a curt bow but stayed where he was.

The sheriff scowled. 'Well, what are you waiting for?'

'There is something that has come to my attention, my Lord,' Flynn began tentatively. 'It is only minor perhaps, and normally I'd report it to Sir Guy, but...'

'Honestly! He might as well have stayed in France, for all the good he's been since he got back!' The sheriff banged his seal into a puddle of melted wax, causing flecks of red liquid to fly across the desk, 'Come on! What is it?'

'It concerns the servant who tends your clerks and offices, my Lord. A responsible position, with access to all your private papers, and even the money store, my Lord.'

'Jerrard?' The sheriff's eyes narrowed. 'He's been here years, what of him?'

'Are you sure, my Lord, that he can be *entirely*, trusted?'

Robin stood still. He'd only got halfway to Herne's cave when the sixth sense he'd developed since living in Sherwood, told him the Lord of the Trees had come to him instead.

As he peered into the tightly grown clump of ash trees ahead, a mist began to seep between the branches. Moving slowly, but with purpose, it seemed to reach out to the outlaw. Curling around Robin's feet, it sent goose-pimples across his flesh, coating him in a clammy cold that was in stark contrast to the heat of the late morning sunshine in which he'd bathed but moments before.

Herne emerged from between the trees.

My son.

Although his lips remained motionless, Herne's words echoed unmistakably through the trees; commanding, clear and controlled. They could have come from the deer headdress he wore, from the soul of the trees, or even from the air itself.

'Herne.' Robin dropped to one knee in deference.

'You have been dreaming of your mother.'

The words were spoken as a fact rather than a question, and even though Robin had long since stopped wondering how Herne always knew the contents of his mind, he was still surprised.

'I have. Can you tell me why?'

The morning breeze increased in pace, wrapping itself around Herne and his son. Leaves danced between them as the spirit replied, 'Sherwood's future will be shaped by your past. A decision awaits you.'

The breeze became stronger, encircling Robin like a warm blanket that smothered away the mist's chill. 'A decision? Huntingdon?'

'The servant will guide and the sons must choose as the Apocalypse rides.'

'Sons.' An image of Sir Guy of Gisburne shot through Robin's mind. *My father's sons or other men's sons?* Instead of voicing the thought, Robin called out, 'Jerrard. He's the servant. But who or what is the Apocalypse? There's nothing but fear and rumour and…'

'You are driven by fear!' Herne's arms rose, both aged hands pointing at Robin. For a split second, the outlaw thought they looked beseeching—or were they levelled in accusation? For the first time, Robin found himself wanting to reach out to Herne, to get closer to his spirit father; but the breeze that surrounded him blended with the mist, becoming a haze; forming a barrier between him as his guide.

'Listen to Mathilda, past, present and future. Something is coming. Follow you heart, as brother fights brother and the kingdom shakes.'

Again, Robin tried to step forward. Immediately the wind spun around him, making his eyes water. Yet the leaves and twigs that battered against his arms, legs and chest didn't so much as scratch him.

'You said sons, and now you say brothers.' Robin voiced the thought he'd been avoiding. 'Do you mean Guy or the brothers of the Order of this Apocalypse? Herne, please! Just this once! Tell me what you mean.'

Herne, his voice rebounding off the shimmering shield around Robin, hurled out his reply. 'I cannot help you. We are distanced by choices.'

'But Herne!'

'Only by being who you *truly* are—in the *heart* and the *blood* and the *soul,* can you vanquish the enemies of England. Make the choice.'

Robin opened his mouth, desperate to ask more questions, but the Lord of the Trees had gone.

The haze that had wrapped around the outlaw dissolved and the breeze dropped in an instant. For three long seconds an eerie silence coated the clearing, before the first few birds were courageous enough to resume their interrupted songs. Robin knocked away some leaves that had settled on his shoulders. He was used to feeling confused after seeing Herne—frustrated and angry even. They were the emotions which drove him, kept him determined to understand his path. This time though, on top of all those feelings, he was worried. He'd sought out the spirit for help and guidance, but all he'd got was an overwhelming sense that he was alone.

Robin sank onto the earth beneath him. It was churned up, as if a gale had laid waste to the area around his feet, but nothing else nearby was disturbed. Every branch swayed happily above him, just as it had before. The sun, sending individual rays of light and heat through the thick canopy above, felt natural—not like the humid heat that had coated him before.

Robin knew it was ridiculous to feel alone as he tried to calm his thoughts. He knew wasn't alone: he had Marion and Tuck, John and Will and Nasir and Much. Never had anyone had such loyal companions as he. And, as a child, he had had Aland, Edgar and Jerrard.

Robin jumped back to his feet and spun around, but there was no one there. At least, there was no one to see. Feeling self-conscious, he whispered, 'Mother?' There was no reply. Sitting back down, tilting his head back, Robin rested against a tree trunk. 'Herne said I should listen to you, but…'

I am in your blood, Robert.

Closing his eyes, Robin muttered, 'Is that really you? How can I hear you?'

You can't. You can feel me.

'I have to make a decision. Huntingdon or Sherwood. Is that the decision Herne means?' Robin ran a hand over his face. He'd been forced to make that choice once before, and he'd always known it would come again—should he outlive his father. He'd never been sure he would, nor was he now. Anything could happen tomorrow—or today. It only took a lucky forester with a well-aimed arrow, or a soldier brave enough to step forward, to end everything.

Be brave, Robert. Do what Herne says. Talk to your own Mathilda.

A rustle to his left made Robin's eyes fly open. His hand had drawn Albion before he'd registered that the approaching threat was no more than a passing rabbit.

He almost sat down again, but instinctively he knew the echo of his mother had gone. Replacing Albion, Robin took his bow from his shoulder and drew an arrow from his quiver, taking the precaution of having it ready to fire. There had been nothing in Herne's warning to suggest he was in imminent danger, but that, along with his impossible conversation with his mother, had made him wary.

'Talk to my own Mathilda,' Robin mused. He would, but first he wanted to speak to Tuck.

CHAPTER 9

Robert de Rainault took a sip of wine and winced. It wasn't bad enough to spit out—after all, it had been a present from the king—but it wasn't good either. Sniffing at the contents of his goblet, the sheriff wondered if John had sent him bad wine on purpose. An additional insult on top of all the others the monarch had flung at him the last time he'd been to check on his shire of Nottingham.

Jerrard? The sheriff wasn't entirely convinced by Flynn's implication of dishonesty concerning one of his oldest servants. But then the sheriff had made it a policy not to believe anything he hadn't seen with his own eyes long before Nottingham became his to control. It was a principle that had, on the whole, served him well.

Tapping his fingers impatiently against the desk before him, de Rainault's eyes landed on the pile of documents still awaiting his signature. There were far more than usual. Most of them were letters from local churchmen in varying fits of panic and outrage about the Interdict and demanding to know what he was going to do about it.

'What exactly do they expect me to do, that's what I want to know? My hands are tied by the king and positively shackled by the Church.' He picked up a letter, poorly scribed, but nonetheless legible, from Father Michael in Edwinstone. The cleric was bleating about three forthcoming weddings. 'It's bad enough I have to deal with Hugo's grumblings, let alone the peasant priests!'

He threw the letter back down. The temptation to chuck them all onto the fire was huge. He'd done that once before with a collection of accounts that had been particularly tedious and showed rather too many signs of not balancing in the Crown's favour. The sheriff grinned as he remembered how much pleasure he'd taken in blaming Gisburne when, inevitably, the king's clerks had noticed the missing missives—or rather had questioned where they were. Gisburne had been puce with rage and humiliation.

De Rainault's smugness dissolved. He wouldn't

be able to get away with such an act a second time, not least because de Rainault had a feeling Gisburne wouldn't put up with taking the blame again—not now. Not since he'd returned from France.

The sheriff took another sip of wine, his expression contorting as the bitter liquid hit the back of his throat. 'What *did* happen to you while you were away, Gisburne?'

He had no chance to think on the matter of his deputy further, for a heavy knock on the door indicated that Jerrard had come as summoned.

'My Lord, Sheriff.' Jerrard bowed as he entered. 'How may I be of assistance?'

Standing up, the sheriff stared along his nose at his servant. 'It has been bought to my attention that you left the castle in the early hours of yesterday without permission and did not get back until dawn.'

'That is correct, my Lord.'

The sheriff looked puzzled, 'You admit it?'

'Forgive me, my Lord. If time had allowed, I would have sought your blessing, but you are a busy man and, at the time of my leaving, would have been abed. I did not wish to disturb you, so I left a message to explain my absence.'

Noting that Flynn had conveniently omitted to mention Jerrard hadn't left the castle in secret, the sheriff asked, 'And what was it that took you from my castle and into Sherwood?'

'My cousin, my Lord. She had been unwell for a while. I was summoned to see her before the chance to do so again in this world was taken from me.' Jerrard kept his eyes fixed on the chain of office that hung around the sheriff's neck. 'So I rushed to Papplewick. The quickest way to get there is to travel through, rather than around, the forest.'

'And yet you returned so soon. Do you have winged feet, Jerrard?'

'Would that I did, my Lord. If I had, then I might have made it to the village in time to be say goodbye, rather than to be greeted by sombre faces.' Jerrard sighed softly, 'I can only apologise again that I did not ask permission from you directly, my Lord.'

'As you said.'

Jerrard could feel the sheriff's unblinking, toad-like eyes on him. His palms prickled. He'd been given the perfect opportunity to speak with him privately, and coughed nervously, his mind filling with images of Mathilda, her son and his master, the earl. Their imagined presence gave him the courage to speak.

'With respect, if I may, my Lord, I have a concern that may be significant. Or perhaps I'm just a foolish old man.'

'A concern?' The sheriff's eyes flashed. 'And what might that *concern* be?'

'I've served you a long time, my Lord. And I—'

The sheriff sat back at his desk and pulled forward the pile of correspondence that awaited his attention. 'Get to the point. What is your concern?'

'I overheard a conversation I was not supposed to hear.'

'Overheard conversations are usually not meant to be heard.'

Jerrard hurried on as the sheriff abruptly stopped fiddling with the pile of paper he'd been fussing over. 'I wasn't listening out for it, my Lord, I was just there and so I heard.'

'Heard what? Spit it out, man!' De Rainault picked up his wine goblet and banged it on the desk. Immediately cursing, as the wine he'd forgotten it contained shot across the paper. 'Damn and blast! Now see what you've done!'

Jerrard had already leapt forward, yanking a pile of papers away from the river of blood-red liquid streaking across the oak surface. Yanking a cloth from the belt of his tunic, he began to soak up the spillage as the sheriff held out his wine-spattered tunic.

'Just look at this! And that wine was from the king! The king!'

'I'm sorry, my Lord, I…'

Jerrard kept dabbing up the unpleasant smelling wine as de Rainault puffed in exasperation, 'Well, at least it's ruined some of these!' He took a handful of blotched documents and threw them onto the fire. 'I can't read them now even if I'd wanted to. The ink has run everywhere.'

Knowing it was best to say nothing, Jerrard waited, hoping the anger radiating off his master's flushed face would fade as quickly as it had arrived.

'This accidental listening…' the sheriff hissed, 'what did you hear and from whom did you hear it?'

'Sir Guy of Gisburne and your captain of the guard, Flynn, my Lord.'

De Rainault stopped fussing with his wine-soaked sleeves and sank slowly into his seat. 'Gisburne *and* Flynn?'

'Yes, my Lord. They were in Sir Guy's chamber. Or rather, Sir Guy was in his chambers. Flynn was on its threshold.'

The sheriff was suspicious. 'Now why would Flynn be visiting Gisburne in his chambers? The mind recoils at the thought!'

'I believe, my Lord…' Jerrard paused, licking his lips. He knew what he was about to say would throw the sheriff into a temper that would make his response to the spilt wine nothing more than a childish tantrum. Men had died for less from the sheriff's rages.

'Come on, Jerrard!'

'I believe I heard Flynn blackmail Sir Guy, my Lord.'

'What?!'

'I said... '

'Yes, I heard you.' A sly smile crossed the de Rainault's face. 'Go on.'

Jerrard dabbed up the last of the wine puddle and stood back from the stricken desk. 'Flynn was clearly displeased that Sir Guy's reappearance meant his ambition to become your deputy was thwarted.'

'You're not telling me anything I don't know, Jerrard.'

'Flynn had seen something in Sir Guy's chamber. I assume that means he must have been in there previously without permission. Anyway, he was asking Sir Guy for money to prevent him from telling you what he knew.'

'And what *does* Gisburne have hidden away?'

'I don't know for sure, my Lord, but a tunic and a scrap of cloth were mentioned.'

'A tunic?' The sheriff's hand came onto the desk with a heavy thump. 'A tunic! I have hundreds of tunics and I'm damned sure Gisburne has, too. Probably some new French fashion item he's proud of but too ashamed to wear in front of me. God knows what personal and private tastes Gisburne has.'

'I'm sure, my Lord, but he still paid the captain.'

'Gisburne *paid* Flynn money to stop him telling me something?' The sheriff sounded genuinely shocked, as he sat back down. But more, Jerrard suspected, by the fact that Gisburne had parted with money, rather than because had a secret. 'And if I went into Gisburne's chamber and demanded to see his tunics, what do you think I'd find?'

'I truly don't know, my Lord. I just thought…'

'Thought! You didn't think at all! If you had, you'd have come straight to me when Flynn took the money… *if* he did…' The sheriff suddenly stopped.

'He did, my Lord, I…'

'It was Flynn who reported your absence to me. He questioned your honesty, Jerrard.'

'My Lord, I have always been honest with you. I am being now.'

'And yet you put your dead cousin before your duty. You should have told me what you'd seen straight away.'

'I know, my Lord. I'm sorry. I was worried about my family and…'

The sheriff's eyes began to twitch as he threw the now-empty goblet at Jerrard. 'Get out! Go on! Get out of here! Seeing as you respect the cook enough to leave messages with him rather than me, you can go and work for him instead of my clerks.'

'But, my Lord Sheriff, I tell the truth. Gisburne has a secret and Flynn knows of it!'

'OUT!'

Jerrard hurried back to his chambers, looking neither left nor right, and sat back on his cot, his heart beating fast. He wasn't sure what to do. Did he wait and see if the sheriff searched the castle, or would he lose interest in what he'd heard once the flush of anger had left him? It was likely that Gisburne would have removed the article in question by now, or at least hidden it where even the sheriff couldn't find it. The servant's mind turned to Flynn. It was interesting that he'd been the one to report his absence to the sheriff. He was obviously more afraid than Jerrard had realised and now the sheriff was suspicious of Flynn as well as Guy. Heaving himself up again, Jerrard pulled his scrip back out from under his cot and headed to the kitchen. He'd work there for an hour, just while he waited to hear if de Rainault had ordered a search of the castle or not. Then, he'd leave.

CHAPTER 10

Robin could hear Tuck's good-natured chuckle and Marion's soothing voice as he approached the camp. They were busy carving the remaining meat from the spit, otherwise it was quiet but for the crackle of the fire. 'Where is everyone?'

'John's gone for a walk with Meg, and Will and Nasir are keeping an eye on the Newark road, in the hope of bagging a few marks from any undeserving travellers.'

'And Much?'

'He's bagging rabbits. Or I hope he is.' Tuck pressed his hands together as if in prayer. 'Last time I sent him rabbiting he didn't catch a thing and we all went hungry.'

'So we did,' Robin smiled, but his thoughts were elsewhere.

'What's wrong?' Marion frowned. 'What did Herne say?'

'It's difficult to explain, but the main thing was about making a choice—a decision—and that I should talk to you. At least, I think he meant you. "My Mathilda" he said.'

Marion's looked surprised, 'Your Mathilda?'

Robin flushed slightly, 'My father said you were like her once.'

'Your father thinks I'm like your mother?' Marion's eyes shone. 'Jerrard spoke so fondly of her; a woman of passion not afraid to stand her ground amongst the men in her life. I'm flattered.'

'In that, you are very alike.' Robin was hesitant as he reached out a hand to her. 'There's something you should know.'

Tuck, who'd been listening, but pretending not to, peered up from the deer carcass he'd been stripping. 'I meant to say, Robin, I want to speak to the parson at St. Matthew's, see if he's heard any more about this interdict. Would this be a good time?'

'Good idea.' Appreciating the friar's tact, Robin said, 'If the interdict happens then you'll be needed a lot around here for weddings, christenings and…'

'Funerals.' Marion ended Robin's sentence. 'Something bad really is coming isn't it? Something other than the Pope taking his petty squabbles with King John out on the people?'

'I think so. Herne said a great deal, but said nothing at the same time.'

Robin's forehead puckered as he explained how the air had felt like it was trapping him in place, binding him to the spot, but that nothing had hurt him. 'I should have been pelted with twigs and leaves, but I wasn't even scratched. It was as if the forest had cocooned me.'

Marion swapped puzzled glances with Tuck, who said, 'Sounds like Sherwood is trying to keep you here.'

'Maybe. It was strange. I got the feeling that something was blocking our connection. It was as if Herne wanted to help me, wanted to tell me more, but he couldn't. A choice, he said.'

'A choice?' Marion looked at Tuck again as he washed his greasy hands in a butt of water.

The friar asked carefully, 'Huntingdon?'

'Oh,' Marion answered before Robin could, her eyes lowering, '*that* choice.'

Drying his hands, Tuck swung his cloak over his shoulders. 'I will leave you to talk.'

'Give the parson my regards.' Robin smiled gratefully at his friend. 'And take some money. He struggles enough to feed his parishioners as it is. He might be glad of some alms.'

Thanking Robin as he went, Tuck bustled into the forest.

'Shall we sit down?' Marion gestured to the fire. 'Or would you rather walk?'

'Let's stay here.' Robin felt anxious as he sat next to the woman he loved. 'There's something I should tell you. Tuck knows, but the others don't. It's important that they never do.'

'But Tuck knows?'

'It was a confession. He is sworn to secrecy of course, but I know he knows, and he knows I know he knows.'

Marion's forehead creased, making her freckles fold into pretty lines on her face. 'Perhaps you should tell me, then.'

'Do you remember when Morgwyn of Ravenscar showed you images in her cauldron, using that enchanted ink?'

As shiver ran through Marion. 'How could I forget? I thought she'd taken you from us forever.'

Robin watched the sway of the flames before them. 'Most of what Morgwyn showed you wasn't real. They were lies to scare you, to make you see things that weren't there.'

Marion shuddered. 'It was the worst kind of cruelty, making me think... making us believe that... Herne spoke to me then, too.'

...for when the eyes come alive.

'Yes.' Robin took hold of her hands, recalling how jealous he'd felt when the sorceress had shown Marion visions of her dead husband. 'But not everything she taunted you with was a trick. One thing was real. A painful truth I was too afraid to share with you however much I wanted to.'

'Why were you afraid to tell me?'

Robin held her eyes, hoping she wouldn't walk away from him. 'Because it concerns my brother.'

'Brother? But you haven't got...' Marion's eyes widened as her words trailed into shocked silence, and the memory of Morgwyn of Ravenscar's hateful taunts about the Earl of Huntingdon rang in her ears.

De Rainault surveyed his deputy's quarters as if he was examining a dung heap. There were piles of discarded hose heaped on a chair, and his bed was unmade. In contrast, a spare uniform hung clean and proud from a nail on the wall, and the spare pair of boots that sat beneath it shone, the leather so polished that the sheriff could almost see his face in the toes.

'I can see why you don't have visitors to your chambers, Gisburne.'

Sir Guy lounged against the wall, his arms folded protectively over his chest. 'To what do I owe the honour, my Lord?'

'Oh you know how it is, Gisburne, every now and then I have a yen to visit every part of *my* castle. Make sure everyone in it is treating it with the care and *respect* it deserves.'

'Indeed, my Lord.' Gisburne glared over the sheriff's shoulder at Flynn, 'Why is *he* here?'

'Because I asked him to come, Gisburne!' the sheriff snapped. The sickly aroma of the spilt wine clung to his robe, making him feel nauseous as well as cross. 'He is here because you, God help him, are his superior and, more to the point, he obeys my orders. Good enough for you, Gisburne?'

'I meant, my Lord, why are we meeting here, in my *private* room.' Gisburne radiated hate in the captain's direction.

Flynn however, had lost his smug expression, and was looking uneasy. *Jerrard has told him. He told the sheriff what he overheard. The miserable wretch!*

Seconds later, the sheriff confirmed Flynn's fear.

'The captain here has got it into his head that you're hiding things from me, Gisburne. Now why would he think that?'

'I can assure you, my Lord…'

'Can you, Gisburne?' De Rainault's eyebrows lifted, 'Ah, well I'm instantly reassured. So, assure me.'

'How, my Lord?'

'By proving that there is nothing hidden in here that shouldn't be.'

Two points of hot colour pinched Guy's pale cheeks as he fought to rein in his rising temper. 'There is nothing here that shouldn't be.'

'Excellent. Then you won't mind Flynn searching the place and making absolutely sure, will you?'

'My Lord! My word should be good enough for you!' Gisburne was outraged. 'After all these years, I would have thought…'

De Rainault raised a hand, speaking in a calm manner that experience told him would enrage Guy more than shouting at him would. 'I live in hope of you having a thought, Gisburne. Who knows? Today might be the day.' He motioned to Flynn to step forward. 'Show me where this tunic is hidden.'

'Tunic, my Lord?' Flynn faltered.

'The one I am informed you have been making Gisburne here sweat over. Demanded money over its existence even.' The sheriff fixed Flynn with a greedy stare. 'You'll go far, Captain Flynn.'

'My Lord, I assure you…' Flynn was looking as uncomfortable as Gisburne now.

The sheriff, however, was enjoying himself immensely. 'We will discuss the matter of blackmail later, Flynn. I have no doubt you'll work out the most sensible means of atoning for such an act.'

'Blackmail, my Lord?' Flynn attempted to appear suitably affronted. 'Who dares to have said such a thing?' He gave a theatrical pause before nodding. 'It was Jerrard, wasn't it? Spreading poison because I caught him leaving his post without permission!'

Flynn caught Gisburne's eye. 'I promise you, my Lord, I've never blackmailed anyone in my life. And I'm sure, if I had, then Sir Guy would have reported the fact to you immediately. *Wouldn't you*, Sir Guy?'

'Without hesitation, my Lord.'

'Of course you would, Gisburne. How remiss of me.' De Rainault's eyes narrowed further as he regarded his two chief men-at-arms. 'And I suppose Jerrard made it all up, and there is nothing hidden in here at all?'

'It would appear he lied to you, my Lord.' Gisburne kept his cold stare on Flynn. 'But why would he do that?'

'Why indeed?'

'Unless…' Flynn chewed his lip, thinking fast to try and save his hide, 'unless he wanted you away from your office, my Lord.'

'Whatever for?'

'Money, perhaps? He has access to the counting room, does he not?'

The sheriff had to resist the urge to applaud his captain's quick thinking. 'Then I suggest you both make haste to my quarters and make sure everything is still there.'

De Rainault waited as neither of his subordinates moved, each eyeing the other with distaste.

'Well, go on then!'

Flynn ran off, his hand already drawing his sword.

'You too, Gisburne. Or do you want the captain stealing all the glory when he catches my coin store being robbed?'

'Aren't you coming, my Lord?' A film of sweat had broken out across Gisburne's forehead as he considered the prospect of leaving the sheriff alone in his room.

'I'll catch you up. Off you go.'

With no choice but to obey, Gisburne raced after Flynn.

The sheriff stood still and smiled. He had to hand it to his captain, he was a devious one. Heading into the corridor, the sheriff called to a maid walking down the stairs with an armful of bed linen. 'You, come here. Take a message to the kitchen. Ask for Jerrard…'

As the young girl scuttled off, muttering the message over and over for fear of forgetting it, the sheriff moved back to the chamber.

'Now then Gisburne, exactly what have you got hidden in here?'

CHAPTER 11

Marion hadn't spoke for a long time.

Robin watched her, wanting to say something, but afraid that anything he did say would be wrong.

She hadn't shouted at him for not telling him before, nor had she cried or declared disappointment in him. She'd just been shocked. He hadn't expected that, not after Morgwyn had paved the way; sowing the seeds of doubt about his paternal connection with Guy. Marion, however, hadn't considered it could be true for a minute. What frightened Robin now was what else Morgwyn might have said to her that she'd previously dismissed, but might now be wondering about.

After what felt like a lifetime, Marion turned to him. 'Margaret of Gisburne. She told Tuck about

Guy when he took her confession, just before she died?'

'Yes.' Robin licked his lips. He was suddenly desperate for a drink but didn't want to move now Marion had started to speak. 'Tuck guessed that Margaret had told me, too. It isn't a matter we've discussed, although whenever we fight Guy, I can feel Tuck's eyes on me.'

Marion threw a stone into the fire. Its smooth surface fizzled before plummeting into the heart of the flames. 'Tuck wouldn't want you to kill your own brother, no matter who he is.'

'I'd rather not kill anyone.' Robin took Albion from its sheath and laid it out on the earth before them.

'I know.' Marion stared at the sword that had once belonged to Robin of Loxley and had been more than earned by Robert of Huntingdon. 'And that's the difference.'

'I'm sorry?'

'That's why were you so afraid to tell me wasn't it? Because you were worried I might think that you're like him... like Gisburne? Well, you're not.' She reached out and stroked his blonde hair, 'Apart from this of course. You are not responsible for your father's actions, Robin.'

'I've killed a lot of men.'

'So has Gisburne. But you've *regretted* every death.' Marion ran a finger over the runes carved into Albion's blade. 'He hasn't. To Guy, the body that hits the ground is forgotten before it falls.'

'I suppose so.'

A grey cloud passed above the canopy, making both outlaws look up as the light that had streamed between the trees faded away. Moving closer to Robin's side, Marion said, 'The story Jerrard told about Edwin. You said he was trying to explain why you couldn't kill Gisburne.'

'Yes.' Robin nodded, 'That's what he said, but…'

'You can't see it, can you?' Marion shook her head. 'Edwin could just have easily been Guy. Edwin was only young, but life had already crippled him, his loss and hurt replaced by unrealistic ambition and jealousy. The sheriff gave him the chance to belittle you in the face of others and Edwin took it to try and make himself appear superior to you. And what did you do?'

'I…'

Marion placed a finger on Robin's lips. 'You took the blame for him. Showed him an act of kindness he didn't deserve because he was your friend. If Guy had grown up as your brother then you would have done the same for him, although, if he had, I don't think he'd have been the man he is today. And the reason for that is his father.'

'We have the same father, that's the problem.'

'No, you don't.' Marion moved her hand to Albion, tracing a finger over each rune. 'Guy was raised by Edmund of Gisburne. A brute and a bully by repute. You were raised by the earl and men like Jerrard. And then you came to the forest and another father claimed you—a different sort of father. A guide, an inspiration to do good, whatever the cost.'

'Herne.' Robin's lips curved up at the corners. 'He can be every bit as frustrating as the earl.'

Marion leaned forward to kiss away his doubts. 'Our fathers were the ones who raised us, influenced us and cared for us, even when we let them down.'

'You chose to leave your father and come back to Sherwood after you'd been pardoned by King John.' Robin found himself counting the freckles on Marion's nose as he added, 'Sir Richard of Leaford was a good man. It can't have been an easy decision for you either.'

'My father would have been in danger if I'd stayed.' Marion gave Robin a tight smile that held a volley of regret. 'I think he was proud of me in his own way. Just as your father is of you.'

Robin placed a palm over her hand as it lay on Albion's hilt, hoping they could draw strength from the blade together. 'Guy is older than me. Whatever the rights and wrongs of his arrival into the world, he *is* my father's son. If Jerrard's instincts are right, and Guy is involved with these Apocalypse knights…'

'You are sure they are that dangerous? That they could find out about Guy's true parentage somehow?'

'Jerrard thinks so, although I don't understand why. Herne has warned me about them to, but I sense it's for a different reason. He couldn't help me. That we are distanced by choices.'

'Which is where our conversation began.' Marion kept her eyes on the sword. 'You said your mother has been talking to you in your dreams. Why not try to think as she would have done? Remember Robin, your father loved your mother. He'd listen to her if she were around to guide him.'

'Just as I listen to you.' Robin stared into the forest before him. 'Life is full of choices. I chose to disappoint my father, give up the earldom and come here. It was a hard choice, but I made it.'

'And now you have to make it again.' Marion hunched her knees protectively up to her chin.

'That's just it though,' Robin's shoulders sagged. 'At first, that's the choice I thought Herne meant, but now, talking to you, I'm wondering if I was wrong. What if that *isn't* the choice he was referring to?'

'What do you mean?'

'Think about it. Even if my father asked me to be his heir again, and I accepted, which I wouldn't, but if I was forced to somehow…, perhaps to keep Guy away from the earldom—how long do you think I'd last before I was made an example of by the king? I'd be dead within a week.'

Marion was quiet for a moment, before she said, 'So is the choice something simpler? Maybe it's whether you go with Jerrard when he gets back, see your father, and to talk to him about his fears for the earldom and Gisburne.'

'Maybe,' Robin let out a puff of regret, 'Whether it is or not, it would be good to heal our differences once and for all.'

CHAPTER 12

He wouldn't have believed it if he hadn't heard it with his own ears. The maid who'd delivered the message, however, was not one to doubt. He'd known her for years; if she'd been cut in half, she'd be honest to the core.

Jerrard wasted no time. Pulling his scrip from where he'd hidden it amongst the sacks of food in the vegetable store, he threw in a handful of carrots from a nearby basket as a gift for Tuck. Then, walking as fast as he could without drawing attention to himself, he made for the servants exit at the back of the kitchen.

Weaving through a bustle of maids, grooms and guards making their way in or out of the castle, Jerrard kept his head high and his eyes and ears alert for trouble. Only when he reached the stable courtyard did he pause for breath. Hooking his bag higher onto his shoulder, he checked to make sure he wasn't being followed.

Leaving the cover of the arched doorway that divided the castles interior from its exterior, Jerrard struck out for the drawbridge which would take him into Nottingham itself. It was a journey he'd made many times before, but now, with the sheriff's warning ringing in his ears, it felt like the longest trek of his life.

Why would the sheriff warn me? Did he find the evidence Robin wanted him to see?

With each step Jerrard took his conviction that he had to get to Huntingdon grew stronger. Pausing again, Jerrard peered into the stable courtyard ahead, his heart racing.

There were several soldiers milling around, but none paid him any heed, so he pushed his shoulders back and walked sedately across the sawdust and hay that patched the gravelled floor. Grooms were busy feeding the horses, while a group of soldiers saddled their mounts before going on patrol. Inhaling the scent of straw, dung and feed, Jerrard realised that it had been years since he'd noticed the smell, and now he'd never smell it again—not here anyway.

Adopting the same route he always took, Jerrard walked around the edge of the stalls rather than across the centre of the courtyard, even though that would have been faster.

Get out of the castle and get to Robin. Rest, then go to Huntingdon.

Repeating these thoughts over and over, Jerrard kept his eyes focused on the portcullis as it came into view.

The passage ahead was all that stood between him and escape into the forest. It was empty but for a hay cart. Its driver had dismounted and was talking to the guard at the gate. From their demeanour, Jerrard suspected they'd spoken many times, probably becoming friends over the years as one delivered the hay and the other allowed the delivery to be made.

Safe in the knowledge that the same guard had seen him pass this way hundreds of times before as well, Jerrard kept going; all the time expecting Sir Guy or Flynn to arrive behind him and accuse him of treachery—or worse—deliver an arrow to his back without wasting breath or demanding explanations.

"Flynn told Gisburne that it was you who told me about the tunic."

The sheriff's warning circled back through his head as he got closer to Nottingham. Flynn was not a man Jerrard had ever wanted as an enemy, but the thought of Gisburne having a grudge against him… The old servant shivered at the consequences as he hurried on.

Will Scarlet had only just sat down. His hand was halfway to the cup of ale Tuck was passing him when Robin and Marion arrived back to camp after electing to take a walk while they worked out what to do next.

'I want you and Nasir to watch for Jerrard.'

'But we only just got back,' Will groaned as he threw a bag of coins to Robin. 'That cloth merchant from Newark, the one who always overcharges when he thinks his customers can't work out their change. He's very sorry about that apparently.'

Robin grunted as he weighed the marks in his hand. 'I bet he is. Well done.'

'But not well done enough to be allowed to rest for five minutes.'

'Sorry, Will.'

'You saw Herne?' Nasir took a drink as he waited for Will to haul himself off the ground.

'I did. And we need to find Jerrard. He should be back from Nottingham.'

'Give him a minute!' Will snapped. 'He's an old man. If he's ransacking the castle for a tunic or, if he was brave enough to tell the sheriff of his suspicions then...'

'He could be in the dungeon.' Nasir frowned.

'He could.' Robin swallowed. 'I didn't like sending him back there, but it seemed the only answer. If the sheriff becomes wary enough to watch Guy more closely, it will have been worth it, but only if Jerrard gets out again.'

'And if he doesn't?' Will tied a water pouch to his sword belt. 'We can't go in and save him Robin, you do know that don't you?'

'I know.' Robin snapped, before taking a steadying breath. 'If Jerrard isn't back by nightfall, I'm going to see my father.'

Will's eyebrows rose. 'Why?'

'Because I promised I would.' Robin raked a hand through his hair. 'But even if I hadn't, I would go. It's about choices. I'll explain later.'

Walking along a wide track used by those aiming for the villages of Sherwood, Jerrard was about a mile from Nottingham when he felt the vibration of hooves across the dry ground. He turned to see a horse pulling a cart coming fast up the road behind him. A moment later, Jerrard realised it was the hay wagon he'd seen at the castle.

It didn't strike him as odd that the hay was still in place until, as it drew close, Jerrard realised with a start that it wasn't the carter driving it. Diving beneath the cover of the trees, the servant pulled his hood over his head. His hands began to shake.

The cart was being driven by Sir Guy of Gisburne.

Before he'd considered the implications of what he was seeing, the sound of another horse's hooves galloping along the road from Nottingham filled the air. This new mount was gaining on the hay cart fast; sending clouds of dust spiralling across the forest floor. Tensing, Jerrard watched from his hiding place. He knew it was Flynn long before the captain's face was visible. Were they looking for him, or were they hunting each other? Jerrard tried to work out which way to go. There was a clearing behind him with a much thicker growth of trees beyond it—a place where a man could hide for hours. But to reach it, he had to risk exposure first. Or he could run forwards, crossing the path to reach the denser undergrowth on the other side of the path.

But if they saw me…

Jerrard could see that Flynn's crossbow was already loaded, and he'd put money on Gisburne having a loaded crossbow to hand too.

You need to see them. You need to be able to report what happens to the Earl.

The decision whether to flee or not was taken out of his hands, when Gisburne unexpectedly reined in his horse, careering the cart around so fast, it screeched; tilting precariously on two wheels. Watching in horror, Jerrard thought it was going to topple over, but miraculously it righted itself.

Gisburne jumped from his saddle and shot at Flynn so fast that the captain's crossbow dropped from his hand like a stone, his body following after it. The sound Flynn made as he hit the forest floor made Jerrard's stomach churn and bile rise in his throat.

Wishing he could blend into the trunk of the tree he'd pushed himself against, Jerrard observed in fascinated horror as, without a word, Gisburne dashed to the fallen guard and dragged him to the cart.

The action of moving the body lifted his cloak, giving Jerrard a glimpse of not one, but two tunics beneath. The first was the plain brown tabard Gisburne wore when he was working within the castle, but beneath that, Jerrard saw a square of black material and the briefest flash of bright yellow. The sight was gone as soon as Guy stood up again.

The palm Jerrard placed over his mouth wasn't enough to disguise the cry of dismay he involuntarily gave out as Guy threw the dead captain into the cart. The words, 'The Knights of the Apocalypse', had escaped his lips before he could stop them,

'Who's there?' Gisburne's unmistakable voice, cut with arrogance, held an air of fear, 'Come on, you dog! Show yourself!'

Jerrard silently cursed as he stood still, hoping Guy had been too involved in the act of murder to work out which direction the sound had come from.

Spinning round, Gisburne grabbed his crossbow, reloading it as he glared in every direction. Jerrard could have sworn the sheriff's deputy had looked right at him before returning to finishing his grisly task; smothering Flynn's body in hay.

Jerrard had hoped he'd get on the horse and ride off, but now his task was over, Gisburne had become motionless, his head lowered, his arms resting on the side of the cart. His lips were moving fast. If Jerrard hadn't known better, he'd have said he was praying.

Seconds later, the sheriff's deputy stood back from the cart, and without caring that someone could come across the cart in the middle of the track, he ran at full pelt in Jerrard's direction.

After that, all the servant knew was pain.

CHAPTER 13

'Here.' Nasir knelt to the fallen servant as Will arrived at his side. 'It was a crossbow.'

Jerrard's eyes were closed. Sweat coated his face as his right hand gripped his left arm just below the shoulder. He could not move. The bolt had gone through the skin, shattering a bone along the way; pinning the old man to the forest floor.

'Is he dead?' Will scanned the area around them for any signs of life.

'No.' Nasir felt tenderly around the wound, the act causing a sharp groan of pain from the fallen servant. 'The bolt is not deep in the ground, I can free it.'

'And his shoulder?'

'Too soon to say.' The Saracen's expression was sombre. 'We need Tuck and Marion.'

'I'll go.' Feeling utterly helpless in the sight of other people's pain, Will ran through Sherwood. *I bet this was Flynn. I bet it was!*

'The sheriff didn't find the evidence he was hunting for, because Gisburne was wearing it. I saw when he killed Flynn.' Jerrard's words were laboured as he stared into the face of the Hooded Man. 'A black tunic with something bright yellow emblazoned across the front- but I only caught a glimpse of that, so...'

'Could have been a sun.' Tuck wiped a damp cloth over his old friend's forehead.

'Why, what's the sun got to do with it?' Scarlet glared through the trees, as if hoping Gisburne would appear so he could finally finish him off.

'Haven't you ever read the Bible, Will?'

'Of course I ain't!'

'Well, there's some that would like to blot out the sun.'

'Or seek to outshine it.' Robin knelt by his old friend. 'I'm sorry, I should never have sent you back.'

'No need, Master Robert. The...' Jerrard gulped as Tuck pulled hard on a cloth that he was wrapping around his shoulder, '...the bolt is gone, thanks to Nasir here. I'll mend.' He gulped again as Tuck fasten the bandage in place. 'It was the sheriff who warned me. He was the one that got me out of Nottingham.'

'De Rainault did?' Will was stunned. 'Why would he help you?'

'You told him your suspicions,' Robin answered before Jerrard could. 'He believed that Guy was hiding something?'

'He didn't say so, but yes. And now Flynn's dead.' Jerrard winced. 'I have lived in the same home as Sir Guy for many years. I have never liked nor trusted him, but I do know him. And one thing I'd have bet my final mark on would be that he'd have gloated over the murder, crowed to Flynn before he shot him. But he didn't. He said nothing. There was no showing off, no arrogant outburst. He just executed him and then… then he prayed. But…'

'Hang on. He *prayed*? Gisburne!?' John turned to Will in amazement, who shrugged. They were both having trouble believing what they were hearing.

'That's what it looked like, but then, suddenly, it was like he knew where I was. He knew exactly where I was hiding.'

'What do you mean?' Robin squeezed the old man's hand to help distract him from the pain.

'Sir Guy leant against the cart and mumbled to himself. I didn't hear what was said. Then he got up and came straight for me at a run. He was like a fired arrow that knew precisely where to aim. Where to find me.'

'What? Like it was magic?' Much had spoken lightly, but as soon as the words left his lips, he wished they hadn't.

'Oh no.' Will groaned, 'No, no, no. I've told you before. I don't want no more to do with magic!'

'I'm sure it wasn't magic, Will.' Sounding calmer than she felt, Marion said, 'Guy is a good soldier. He could have heard you, Jerrard, or seen your tracks.'

'He could have,' Jerrard conceded. 'Perhaps I imagined it. It's all so hazy now.'

Tuck sat back on his haunches. 'You just rest, my friend. That shoulder is going to take time to mend, so you stop worrying about Gisburne. You can leave that to us.'

'I can't. Time is so short now.' Jerrard spoke urgently. 'Huntingdon. We must go, Master Robert. If Gisburne did know where I was hiding, then perhaps…'

Tuck caught Robin's eye and saw that they shared the same fear. If there *was* magic involved here, then Guy might find out the earl's secret after all.

'I'm going to Huntingdon.'

'But Robin?' Little John's forehead creased, 'You can't. Something's wrong here. The locals are afraid. Wickham is full of it. If the interdict comes, and the alms from the churches stop, and we're not here for the people as well, then…'

'I said *I'm* going, not that we were *all* going.' Robin turned back to Jerrard. 'I promised you I'd see my father, and so I will.'

'I'll come too, Master Robert.'

'No, Jerrard.' Tuck spoke before Robin had the chance. 'You are staying here until the risk of fever has passed.'

'I have no fever, I'm fine.'

'You have a hole in your shoulder and you are, forgive me, not a young man.' Tuck spoke with all the authority of a churchman in a pulpit. 'A journey now would be unwise.'

Robin nodded. 'Tuck's right. I'd hate to lose you, too.'

Jerrard's head sank back against the forest floor. 'Tell the Earl *everything* I told you. Remind him of Edwin. Explain what really happened and why you defended that boy all those years ago. Tell him the sheriff helped me in the end. That de Rainault is wary, but he doesn't know why. Tell him about Guy and…'

Abruptly, the servant stopped talking. The sky had gone dark. Jerrard heard the drawing of swords as, acting on unspoken instinct, the outlaws surrounded him.

A moment later the swords were lowered as a familiar voice coated the grey sky.

Sherwood is troubled. Heed me, Hooded Man. All here will need you when the monks take arms and the sons suffer. Time has run out. You cannot stop an arrow in flight, but you can move its aim. It is time to choose. To make the right choice.

Herne was gone before anyone knew if he'd really been there, or if they'd heard a reflection of a prophecy delivered from afar. The dark snapped away and the sun shone as though it had never stopped.

Will looked at John. 'Is it me, or do you get the impression that Herne doesn't want Robin to leave Sherwood right now?'

CHAPTER 14

De Rainault wasn't often pleased to see his brother, but the arrival of Abbot Hugo in Nottingham castle's great hall was, for once, opportune.

The abbot was immediately suspicious, 'Why?'

'I want to talk to you about Gisburne.'

'Whatever for? He's your problem, not mine. Always has been. And been a waste of space for years, too.'

The sheriff grunted, 'Do you remember Jerrard, one of my chief servants?'

'No. Why should I?'

'Honestly, Hugo, do you ever answer a question without asking another in return?' The sheriff rolled his eyes. 'Jerrard has worked for me for years. He came to see me. To warn me about Flynn and Gisburne.'

'Warn you?'

'You're doing it again!' the sheriff snapped. 'The point is, since Jerrard spoke to me, both Flynn and Gisburne have gone missing.'

'Missing?'

'For Heaven's sake, Hugo!'

Marion wrapped an extra blanket over Jerrard as Tuck fussed over him in the back of the cart they'd borrowed from Wickham.

'Remember what I said. Knock on the side of the cart three times if you need Little John to stop so you can rest. That shoulder should not be jarred more than necessary.'

'I'll be fine, Brother, but thank you.'

Leaving his patient, Tuck went to Marion's side. He could see her watching Robin as he practiced his archery. 'You know, don't you?'

'Yes.'

'I'm sorry, Little Flower. I wanted to tell you but I couldn't.'

Marion laid a comforting hand on Tuck's arm. 'The secrets of a confessional are confidences I'd never ask you to share,'

Tuck looked across the camp. John and Much were gathering some food and drink for their long journey. Meanwhile Will and Nasir sat quietly; each immersed in his owns thoughts as they sharpened their daggers in the firelight. Robin was stood, set back from them all, his bow drawn. Tuck could see his arm beginning to shake; he'd held the bowstring back for too long. When Robin finally let go of the string, the arrow hit the tree he'd been aiming for with a thud that sent crows cawing into the sky.

'Is he alright?'

'Frustrated, I think,' Marion grimaced. 'It wasn't an easy choice for him to decide to make things right with his father. But, once he'd made that choice, he wanted to go immediately. Jerrard is so sure the chance for them to resolve their differences is running out. And now he can't go because he feels he'll be letting Sherwood down if he does.'

'Robin said he thought the forest was trying to keep him here when he spoke to Herne before Jerrard was hurt.' Tuck wiped perspiration from his brow. 'The choice Herne mentioned, do you think it was this one? To stay in Sherwood or to go with Jerrard?'

'Possibly.' Marion sighed, 'but Robin had the sense that Herne couldn't help us until whatever choice he meant has been made.'

'And once it has been?' Tuck watched as Robin fired another arrow. '*If* Gisburne is with these knights and he finds out, then…'

'I know.'

'Something showed Gisburne where Jerrard was hiding.' Tuck felt uneasy, 'I know Jerrard said he made a noise, but the man is a professional spy. He's remained hidden in Nottingham castle since before we lived there. He does not give himself away that easily.'

Marion felt worried, but all she said was, 'Jerrard will tell the earl. He'll explain about our fears over Guy and tell him that Robin wanted to be the one to tell him, but couldn't.'

'I'm not sure it will help if the earl thinks Robin chose the forest over him again.'

'If Jerrard explains Robin was detained by duty he'll understand.' Marion followed Tuck back to the cart to say their goodbyes. 'Obligation to position is something every nobleman is taught to respect from an early age. Whether they like it or not.'

Abbott Hugo saw him first. Nudging his brother's elbow as they sat, side by side, at the high table, they watched as Sir Guy of Gisburne strode into the hall, tugging off his riding gloves as he entered.

'Where the devil have you been, Gisburne?' The sheriff gripped his knife as his deputy approached.

'I bring sobering news, my Lord.'

'Do you indeed?' De Rainault caught the abbot's troubled expression out of the corner of his eye. 'And what news is that?'

'Flynn, my Lord. He's dead.'

The sheriff lowered the goblet he held to the table slowly, but he kept his meat knife to hand. 'Is he? And how did this tragedy occur, Gisburne?'

'Murdered, my Lord. An arrow.'

Reflecting on everything the sheriff had told him about Jerrard's suspicions and his subsequent and unfruitful search of his deputy's room, Abbott Hugo spoke with unusual care. 'In Sherwood, I suppose?'

'It has to have been Robin Hood or one of his dogs, my Lord Abbot.'

'Does it?' De Rainault's eyes shone. 'How convenient.'

Letting the sheriff's sarcasm wash over him, Gisburne continued. 'I instructed some of my men to bring the body to the chapel, my Lords.'

'How forward thinking of you Gisburne.' The sheriff got to his feet. 'And where did my captain meet his end, exactly.'

'He was found by villagers near Papplewick, my Lord.'

'That wasn't what I asked, Gisburne.'

Sir Guy's eyes met the sheriff's. 'I imagine he died where he was found, my Lord.'

'Imagining and thinking.' De Rainault's eyes narrowed. 'France had quite an effect on you.'

Gisburne ignored the jibe. 'There is something else, my Lord.'

'Oh, do tell, Gisburne.'

'Your man, Jerrard. The one Flynn had reason to complain of. He's gone missing.'

The abbot's eyes narrowed, 'Has he, by God?'

'Yes, my Lord. Flynn was found near Papplewick. The man Jerrard had kin there.'

'So he did,' Robert de Rainault replied slowly. 'Are you telling me that Jerrard went to Robin Hood and asked him to dispatch Flynn for him?'

'Flynn is not popular with the outlaws, my Lord.'

'Not *popular?*' the abbot spluttered, 'He's the captain of the sheriff's guard, man! If he was popular with outlaws, he'd have been doing a damn poor job of it.'

'And he didn't do a poor job.' The sheriff's gaze levelled on his deputy, wondering who it was that had taught him to think strategically. Whoever it was, the sheriff wished Guy had met them earlier. Robin Hood might well have been vanquished long ago if he had. 'Flynn was the best captain we've had in years. You didn't like that, did you, Gisburne?'

'My lord, I…'

Twisting on his heels, not giving Sir Guy time to reply, the sheriff moved away from the table, 'Come Hugo.'

'Where to?'

'The chapel.' The sheriff looked back at Gisburne. 'Flynn was my captain. We should pay our respects.'

Reinforcing the importance of not drawing attention to themselves on their journey, Robin watched with the others as John, Much and Jerrard, the latter cushioned in the cart behind them, rode towards Huntingdon.

'However vigilant we have been before, however watchful, we must be even more careful now.'

'What do you want us to do, Robin?' Will's eyes remained focused on the precise spot where the cart had been.

'Get ready.'

'For what?'

'Trouble.'

The temperature in the chapel always felt lower than in the rest of the castle. Today it felt icy. The sheriff was not surprised when he felt his flesh shiver as he stood over Flynn's body.

'An arrow, that's what Gisburne said.'

The abbot nodded. 'You can see where it went right through him.'

'Just shows how little you know about the battlefield, Hugo. An arrow didn't do that. It was a crossbow not a longbow that delivered this wound.'

'So it wasn't Robin Hood?'

'I never thought it was, and neither did you brother,' the sheriff growled.

'What do we do?' The abbot's eyes flicked to the closed chapel door behind them, 'We have no evidence to accuse Guy of Flynn's murder.'

130

De Rainault chewed on his lip as he mused, 'And we would need evidence this time, especially if Jerrard was right about Gisburne's change of allegiance.'

'Do you think he is with the Apocalypse knights?'

'I don't know, Hugo. We haven't even heard that they officially exist yet.'

Hugo snorted, but gave no useful response as the sheriff went on.

'Gisburne has never been very brave. Flynn was though.'

'But Gisburne has always been easily led.'

'True.' The sheriff shivered. 'Come on, Hugo. It's freezing in here. No wonder you churchmen drape yourselves in velvet and fur.'

'What are you going to do about Gisburne, Robert?'

'Watch him.'

'And in the meantime?'

'Prepare for trouble.'

CHAPTER 15

It felt good to be doing something. The waiting, not knowing what was coming, was making Robin edgy, and he knew Will was feeling the pressure of inaction even more than he was.

Sitting in the bows of the oak, his legs tucked up, his body crouched ready to jump when the time came, Robin reflected on what Herne had told him. He'd said that Sherwood's future would be shaped by Robin's past and that the servant would guide. That *had* to mean Jerrard. Robin frowned as he watched the forest. Did Herne know Jerrard would remind him of Edwin so he'd see the similarities between him and Guy? Or, when he talked about his past, did Herne mean his parents? Robin exhaled slowly. All of Herne's prophecies were challenging, but this time he felt as if the sprit was leading him in circles.

A decision awaits me—is that the choice Herne referred to, or are the decision and the choice different things? Why does everything always come back to my inheritance?

His eyes scanned the track to his left. It was empty. If it had been market day, all manner of men and women, children and animals would be walking along, chatting and laughing as they went. His people. The people he helped.

I couldn't help anyone from Huntingdon except those who don't deserve it.

The thought eased the tension in his shoulders as a vision of his mother's face appeared in his mind's eye. He heard her voice echo in his head: *I am in your heart and your blood and your soul.*

In response, he thought: *My mother would stay. She'd stay and help. Even if father needed her, even though she loved him – Mathilda of Huntingdon would stay.*

Knowing in his heart he was right about his mother, Robin whispered a prayer to Herne to protect John, Much, Jerrard and his father.

A bird call from somewhere to his right dragged Robin from his thoughts. It had in fact come from Nasir, who had been watching the road out of Nottingham.

Robin readied himself to jump to the ground as another bird call came: its distinctive sound informing them it was Gisburne who headed their way. He swallowed his sigh of relief. He'd thought Gisburne might come back to see if Jerrard was dead—but he hadn't been absolutely sure. Guy wasn't so easy to second guess these days.

There was a third call. Nasir was telling them that Gisburne travelled alone.

Leaping to the ground, Robin acknowledged Marion as she landed at his side. Together they backed under the cover of the trees. As Robin drew Albion, Marion eased back her bowstring. On the floor of the clearing was the bundle of cloaks they'd placed there, rolled together in the rough shape of a man. A crude, but hopefully effective lure, to make Gisburne believe Jerrard still lay where he'd shot him.

Robin couldn't see Nasir, but he knew he was there, a knife in each hand—just in case. Meanwhile, Tuck was ready on the opposite side of the cluster of trees, his quarterstaff ready to knock Guy into a temporary sleep if Robin said so.

Robin glanced up at Will. He'd angled himself in the tree directly above; poised ready to jump on top of their quarry, toppling him to the ground. Robin could feel his fury radiating down on him from above. Will hadn't taken kindly to being told—yet again—that he couldn't kill Gisburne.

He could hear Guy nearing the clearing. His breathing was so distinctive. An unexpected ripple of regret shot though Robin.

I'm going to have to kill him one day.

We all have to make choices. Herne's voice echoed through his mind

'*That's* the choice?'

Robin's voice had been no more than a whisper, but it had been enough for Marion to look at him in surprise, but there was no time to react. Sir Guy of Gisburne had arrived in the confined space.

If they hadn't seen him so often, Robin realised they might not have known it was Guy. There was no sign of his uniform, instead he wore a plain brown tunic and faded hose, with a black cloak. Over his head, he wore a worn leather hood.

'Now!' Robin had shouted the order, but there had been no need. Will was already flying through the air, knocking their enemy to the ground, as Herne shot a fresh warning through the back of Robin's mind.

The decision between what is best and what is right. That has always been the choice.

Stepping forward, Robin pointed Albion at a spluttering Gisburne's forehead. 'Hello, Guy. Looking for someone?'

As his friends gathered around, each aiming their weapons at the deputy's head, Robin saw a flash of Guy's golden hair as the hood he wore fell back.

He's so like Edwin was.

'Wolfshead!' Guy spat the word, staring hatred at those surrounding him.

Robin crouched down and tugged the covering fully away from Gisburne's face. 'It takes more than a hood to survive in the forest.'

'So what does it take then, Huntingdon?'

Will kicked Guy hard in the ribs, 'Well, it ain't shooting an old man in cold blood.'

'You can't prove it was me, you scum!'

The inevitability of Guys' reaction to being captured by them saddened Robin. 'Your denial merely confirms your guilt, Gisburne. As would Jerrard, if he was here to accuse you.'

Their prisoner opened his mouth to protest, but Robin put his hand up to stop him. 'I really wouldn't bother, Guy. We know you shot him in the shoulder. A poor shot for you. I would have thought your skills would have been honed in France, but it seems you've lost your touch.'

'Don't taunt me Wolfshead, or you will regret it.'

'There are many things I regret, Guy, but at least I can say attempting to murder a loyal servant in the forest and murdering the sheriff's captain, before blaming it all on someone else, is not one of them. I assume you did try to blame at least Flynn's death on me?'

Paling slightly as he thought about the sheriff and the abbot viewing Flynn's body and working out that the wound did not match an arrow, Guy spat, 'No need, not when you have so many other deaths lined up ready to hang you! You! An earl's son.' His expression screwed up in scorn and resentment. 'They still call you that you know. Robin Hood— the *earl's* son. Like it makes what you're doing better because your father is who he is! You don't deserve it. You don't deserve any respect at all!'

Scarlet kicked Gisburne harder, shouting at Robin. 'How can you let this man live? He is one of the worst examples of humankind. He's…'

'A coward.' Marion interrupted, the softness of her voice and the certainty in her tone was more powerful than Will's rage. 'What have you got yourself into this time? You're afraid of something aren't you, Guy?'

'Says the Lady Wolfshead, who hides behind her men, like a…'

Will didn't have the chance to kick Gisburne again because in one swift move, Robin had bent to the floor, dragged him to his feet and slammed him against the nearest tree. His face close to Guy's, he hissed, 'If you ever—*ever*—insult Marion again, I will forget all my principles and kill you right now.'

'I…'

'You do remember principles, Guy? I'm sure you must have had some once.'

Seeing Robin's blade pricking the skin of Guy's throat, Tuck moved forward. As they stood together, he could see a likeness he hoped Gisburne would never see. Placing a hand on Robin's shoulder, Tuck said, 'Honour, kindness and, as you mentioned Sir Guy, respect. Can you still manage those qualities? Knightly qualities they say, although these days the evidence of that is in poor supply.'

'What would you know of honour, Friar?'

'More than you!' Will's temper was, as always, dangerously close to boiling over.

All of a sudden, Guy smiled. It was a creeping grin, unnerving in its brilliance, which made his whole body relax. A confidence radiated from him which no one surrounded by outlaws with weapons should feel. 'It makes no difference if you kill me or not. It never has.'

'Then we'll kill you,' Will snarled.

Robin, aware of Tuck's light but restraining hand, said, 'If it makes no difference, then I suspect it would be crueller to let you live.'

'Why doesn't it make a difference?' Marion asked, seeing the cloud of concern on Tuck's face. She felt it was important to keep Guy talking, although she wasn't sure why.

'Because *they* are coming and nothing you will do or have ever done will matter anymore.'

A tremor of unease shot through Robin. 'The Knights of the Apocalypse. Jerrard was right, you *are* one of them.'

Gisburne said nothing as his eyes met Robin's, his countenance sharp and unblinking.

'If he's one of them, whoever they are, then we need to finish him. We have to!' Will glared at their prisoner. 'Well, Robin?'

Gisburne laughed. 'Your bully boy never did grasp the idea of honour, but perhaps it's time to prove that I understand it. The concept was taught to me by my father, as was the ability to ignore it when it became... inconvenient.'

'Prove it how?' Robin tilted his head to one side

'A sword fight. Isn't that what our fathers would do? The men who taught us to be *so* honourable.'

'Alright.' Robin took a step back. 'The winner is the first to knock his opponent to the ground.'

'No, Wolfshead. The winner is the one who still breathes.'

CHAPTER 16

Jerrard leant against Little John, glad of the big man's support as they stood under the trees at the back of Huntingdon castle.

'Master Robert played here.' He pointed to his left. 'You see that tree there, the one with the low hanging branch twisting to the right?'

'The one with the really thick trunk?'

'That's it, Much.' Jerrard smiled. 'That was the first tree Master Robert climbed. It became his favourite. Whenever his father was cross with him he'd hide in it.'

John grinned as he pictured the young Robin Hood in the making. 'He was up there a lot then.'

'Nearly every day once Mathilda was taken from us. I must go inside.'

Much patted the horse's neck, 'Do you want us to come too, Jerrard?'

'Thank you, Much, but it might not be safe. The earl is a good man, but who knows who is with him.'

John nodded. 'We'll wait here until first light. We can sleep in the cart. But at dawn, we must leave.'

'I will be back before then. Hopefully with a message from the earl to take back to Sherwood.'

The bandage at his shoulder pulled as he walked. The wound was weeping, and the cloth Tuck and Nasir had so tenderly applied had stuck to his broken flesh, making Jerrard wince as each step jarred him.

Although John and Much had made sure he'd had enough food and water, the bumps and jolts of the journey had taken their toll. Light-headed, Jerrard was afraid he'd pass out before he reached the castle's kitchen entrance.

'I must speak to the earl. I must. For Master Robert. For Mathilda... I must...'

The old servant made it as far as the kitchen's spice store before his legs buckled under him. The world spun as he sank to the floor, his senses taken from him as his head glanced against the cold stone.

'My Lord?'

Jerrard sat up, instantly regretting the speed of the move as the room swam and dots formed before his eyes.

'Gently now.' The earl reached out to his oldest servant. 'My physician tells me your wound is severe, but you are lucky in that it isn't infected. Only rest and regular cleaning and changing of your wound will heal you. Your head has a small cut, but nothing that should trouble you beyond a headache.' He patted the servant's good arm. 'Now I have reassured myself you are back with us, I should let you rest.'

'Thank you, my Lord, but I have news which cannot wait.'

The earl lowered himself back into his chair. 'Then tell me.'

'First, my Lord, how long have I been here?'

'A few hours. My man, Camville, found you and settled you safely here. Why?'

A moan of relief escaped from Jerrard's lips. 'Good, then we still have time.'

'Time?'

'Your son saw my delivery to Huntingdon. His men are here, in the forest. They await my word before they return.'

'Robert?' Hope and disappointment crossed the earl's face at the same time. He seemed to age before Jerrard's eyes. 'But he is not here himself?'

'Until an hour before we left, he was coming, but then his duties prevented him. I should say, my Lord, he was ill-pleased that he couldn't be here with me.'

The earl grunted. 'That I doubt.'

'My Lord,' Jerrard licked his dry lips, 'I am an old man now, and I have, I hope, served you well these past decades.'

'You have. And Lady Mathilda before me.'

'Then perhaps, you may permit me to speak candidly? I would not ask such a boon if I did not believe it important, my Lord.'

Huntingdon levelled his grey eyes on his spy. 'I know you would not. Tell me what brings you from Nottingham, wounded, and in the care of my son's men.'

Resting his head on the cushions someone had left for his comfort, Jerrard spoke of his overheard blackmail conversation and how, subsequently, Guy had killed Flynn and shot him.

'Guy did this to you?' A groan, which the Earl would never have allowed himself to make in any company other than Jerrard's, filled the tapestry-covered chamber. 'Sometimes I think it is a mercy his mother passed away. Lady Margaret would be so ashamed.'

'There is more, my Lord.'

'Go on.'

'You have heard of the Knights of the Apocalypse?'

Marion bit her lip. She knew what she wanted to say, but also knew it was pointless to say it. As her eye caught Tuck's, she could see he was also battling with the desire to voice his misgivings—but he too held his tongue. Will, however, was making it very clear that he thought one final fight with Gisburne was long overdue, and he was in no doubt who would be victorious.

While Nasir, swords drawn, watched over Guy, Will buzzed around Robin like an irritated wasp.

'Just do us all a favour and finish him this time.'

Robin, his eyes never leaving his opponent, whispered, 'I told you I don't want to kill him.

'But you ain't got no choice. He has given you no choice! If it ain't him dead on the floor, it's you!'

'There's always a choice, Will. And in the end it's my decision.'

A flash of fear crossed Will's face and he dropped his voice to a whisper. 'What do you mean? You ain't gonna let him win, are you? He's…'

'More useful to us alive.'

'You've said that before. I'm not sure it was true then and I ain't convinced it's true now!'

Robin patted Will on the shoulder. 'I've never said that Will. That was someone else.'

Will flushed the colour of his name, 'Oh, yes… Look… I…'

'It's alright, Will. Nothing's forgotten. Nothing is ever forgotten.' Robin picked up his sword. 'It's time.'

A flutter of soot skittered down the chimney making the fire spark. Jerrard chuckled as the earl complained of how often birds got caught in the flues, sending smuts across the castle floor; sometimes getting themselves roasted in the process.

'The sheriff has the same problem in Nottingham.'

'You were saying that de Rainault has his suspicions about Guy being involved in this so called Holy Order of fighting knights?'

'He made a show of disbelieving me, of course, but the sheriff was curious enough to have Sir Guy's room searched, and worried enough for my safety to send a message warning me to flee.'

The earl looked at his retainer with pride. 'Your worth is shown to me once more, Jerrard. To have made yourself trusted by the man upon which you spy, that's a rare skill.'

'Thank you, my Lord.' Jerrard felt the pressure of time as he went on, 'Do you remember how Lady Mathilda would tell me to trust my instincts?'

'Very well.'

'Then, my Lord, trust me when I tell you that every instinct in my being tells me that you need to see Master Robert.'

This time the earl's sigh made the candles gutter. 'The last time I spoke with my son, we left more estranged than ever.'

'When he came here to apologise for his behaviour after Morgwyn had played with his mind?' Jerrard watched the earl as he added, 'That sorceress made him doubt everything.'

147

'She did, and I understood and forgave that. I told him so.'

'And then you told him he had to expect such things to happen if he chose to live as a rebel.'

'It's the truth!' the earl snapped.

'An unhelpful truth, my Lord.'

'I had to raise a boy to be an earl, not a child to be loved. It's how it has to be. I do wish though, that…' Huntingdon threw his hands up in exasperation. 'I don't know. Every time Robert and I make a fragile truce, something breaks it.'

Jerrard persisted. 'Sir Guy, when he shot me… it was like he knew where I was without seeing me. What if these knights have a power like Morgwyn's? A force of some kind that's helping them?'

'Magic?'

'Maybe.' Jerrard hesitated, framing his question carefully. 'If they do, and *if* Guy is one of them, then should they find out who he is… who he *really* is… then…'

'My God!' If the earl had been pale before, he was white as a ghost now. 'But you aren't sure? You can't prove Guy has joined these people. Even if he has, would he be important enough for them?'

'The son of Edmund of Gisburne is not such a bad prize for them, my Lord.'

148

Jerrard did not need to finish what he was thinking. The earl did it for him. 'But the son of the Earl of Huntingdon—even a bastard son...'

'Especially when the inheritance of his lands and title are in question, my Lord.'

Getting up, the earl began to pace the room. 'But Guy doesn't know. It would be impossible for him to know. Only you and Robert and Tuck know.'

'And the Lady Marion.'

'Of course.' The Earl wiped a hand over his forehead. 'His own Mathilda.'

Jerrard swallowed, the act causing him to wince as he moved his neck. 'Even if Guy doesn't find out, even if these knights never know, you need to make your peace with Robert before it's too late.'

'Before I die.'

'We are neither of us young men, my Lord. Do you really want to leave this realm without resolving your differences with your son? Don't you want to talk to him about the next Earl, discuss with him who you could petition the King to replace you when the time comes?'

'You think King John will listen to me?' The earl picked up a candle, and moved it closer to his old friend, casting a shadow across the room. 'He'll move in his latest favourite and have to live with the consequences.'

'Maybe, but you owe it to England, your conscience, and your son to try.'

'He is reckless! His mother's son.'

'And is that such a bad thing, my Lord?' Jerrard met the earl's eyes. 'Did you not love Mathilda more than any other? If life had not robbed her from you, would she be pleased with your family's current situation?'

'If Mathilda was alive, Robert might not have gone to the forest.'

Leaning forward as much as his wounds would allow, Jerrard dared, 'If Lady Mathilda were alive, my Lord, she might have gone with him.'

'Ah, that she might.' The earl gave a sad laugh. 'I regret that...'

'With respect, my Lord,' Jerrard interrupted, 'age does not give time for regret. There are things I wish I'd said to Edgar and Aland before they'd been taken from us. I always thought there would be more time, but then one day, there wasn't.'

The earl barely heard. His mind was with his wife. 'God knows childbirth is dangerous, but if I'd known I'd never speak to Mathilda again that day...'

'Then please,' Jerrard pleaded, 'speak to Robert. Don't regret not speaking to him too. He lives a dangerous life. You don't know when he'll…'

'Please, Jerrard.' The earl shook his head, 'There is no need to remind me of that. I think of the possibility every day. I will see Robert. Although, if we argue…'

'Then you'll argue. I'm not saying you should pretend to agree with the boy, but he feels the gulf between you, and it troubles him deeply.

'Very well, Jerrard you have made your point well.' The earl rose to his feet. 'I will talk to Robert. Perhaps it is time we spoke as father to son, not earl to outlaw.'

CHAPTER 17

The clash of metal on metal rang through Sherwood. Nothing else could be heard. Even the breeze had stopped, rendering the branches motionless as outlaw and soldier met beneath the trees.

Robin had spoken to his friends before they'd begun. Whatever happened they were not to interfere, not to help him if he looked as if he was going to lose. It had to be a fair fight. His honour was at stake.

Marion slipped her arm into Tuck's, his sturdy bulk as comforting now as it had always been. She could feel Will bristling, his expert eye on every block and parry as the men danced with a speed that was heavily laced with hate on one side and principles on the other.

She wondered if Tuck was thinking as she was.

Similar heights, similar builds, the same hair, albeit different lengths... It's amazing no one noticed before. Or am I only seeing it because I know..?

Tuck drew her closer as Robin's sword landed awkwardly against Gisburne's, and he staggered. For the briefest moment it appeared that the outlaw would fall, but he had righted himself before a gasp of fear had the chance to form in Marion's throat.

She wanted to close her eyes, but at the same time she daren't look away.

On the opposite side of the clearing Nasir watched, his face as impassive as ever. His hands however, gave him away. Each time one of Robin's thrusts or strikes was off-kilter, his fists clenched. Marion could tell he was desperate to draw his own sword, just for the comfort of having something to hold. But Robin had also made them promise not to use any weapons. Marion suspected he knew Will would disobey him. If Robin fell, Gisburne would never leave the forest alive.

Much eased his knife through the stick in his hand, sharpening the end to a satisfying point. He already

153

had a pile of similarly prepared sticks next to him, as he sat crossed legged next to the cart.

The sound of Little John's snoring rattled behind him. The big man had muttered something about not getting enough sleep since he got married, and so Much had offered to stay on watch first. Happy with his own thoughts as he made the skewers for Tuck to use next time he cooked with the spit, Much was just allowing himself the indulgence of reminisces about his few precious months with Kate before she'd been taken from him,[4] when the sound of someone approaching sent him to his feet. Grabbing his bow, he drew back the string, only to lower it again as he saw a very special visitor approach, alone and clearly troubled.

'Little John!' Much raced to the back of the cart, shaking his friend's leg. 'Wake up! It's the Earl of Huntingdon. John!'

'What? Meg?'

'No, John. It's me, Much. The earl's 'ere.'

Leaving John to come to his senses, Much raced back to the front of the cart. 'My Lord.' He gave a clumsy bow. 'Little John's 'ere too, my Lord. He's just coming.'

---

4   See *The Meeting Place*, written by Jennifer Ash. Also available in audio format, starring Peter Llewellyn Williams, Sheila Ham and Barnaby Eaton-Jones.

Smiling at the effort the youngest outlaw was making, Huntingdon held up a hand to him. 'It's alright, Much. I came to thank you for bringing Jerrard home safely. He would have come to see you himself, but I've handed him over to the care of my man, Camville, and my physician.'

Little John hurried into view; brushing down his straw-covered hose as he came to Much's side. 'Thank you, my Lord. Robin will be glad to know of his friend's safety.'

'My son... he is well?'

'He is, my Lord.' John, equally out of his comfort zone as Much when it came to conversing with the nobility, added, 'Bit troubled perhaps.'

'Troubled?'

'He's bothered about this interd... intedee...'

'You mean the interdict, Much,' the earl scowled, 'and so he should be. Sometimes I wonder what the Pope and the King...' Huntingdon broke off, letting his personal fears remain unspoken. 'I have a message for my son. Would you deliver it for me?'

'With pleasure, my Lord.' John dipped his head in what might have been a bow or him simply moving closer so he didn't miss a word of the earl's message.

'I'd like to see him. We have much to discuss.' The earl stared back over his shoulder towards the castle.

'But I can't come to Sherwood, not now. When the interdict is declared, I'll have priests to appease and no doubt the king will come bellyaching to me about the unfairness of the Pope, while the Pope will send an envoy asking me to intercede with the king.'

'Your hands are going to be full, my Lord.' John felt some sympathy with the earl, whose tone suggested he'd rather climb in the back of the cart and sleep all the way to Sherwood.

'They always are, John.' Huntingdon gave a half smile. 'Tell my son I wish to talk to him, that Jerrard speaks sense, and that he is, and always will be, Mathilda's son—and mine. Will you say that—those precise words?'

'We will, my Lord.' John spoke the words back to the earl, to reassure the man that they had been clearly understood. 'Please bid farewell to Jerrard.' The outlaw looked up at the sky. 'If we leave now, we can get home earlier than hoped.'

'Then I bid you well, John, Much.' The earl held out his palm, surprising and confusing the outlaws by shaking their hands. 'And thank you. Thank you for looking out for my son.'

Perspiration glistened off Guy's forehead. Robin could see it shining in the dying light. He imagined his own brow looked similar. He could feel perspiration running down his neck and back. His arms ached and his knees were increasingly aware that they'd been fighting for over an hour, neither one of them ahead of the other. Perfectly matched in skill and fitness.

Brother will fight brother

As he parried another well-aimed clash of their swords, Robin found himself recalling the first time Herne had used those words. They'd been near the sanctuary of St Ciricus. He'd just discovered the truth of Gisburne's patronage.

Now Herne had used similar words—and here he was—*brother against brother*.

Guy's next blow came from the left, almost wrenching Albion from Robin's hand. Realising his focus had been wavering, Robin gathered himself, knowing that he had to end this soon. Sweat was making his palm slippery. It would only be a matter of time before one of them dropped their sword. With a sudden burst of speed, Robin pushed Guy backwards.

Gisburne's face was screwed into a fury of concentration, and although he was moving in the direction Robin dictated, there was no sign of him weakening.

Tuck passed Marion the water pouch. She felt guilty drinking when she knew how thirsty Robin must be, but her mouth was dry with tension. Surely one of them had to win soon. And she needed it to be Robin. Sensing her growing concern, Tuck turned to her.

'He'll win, Little Flower.'

As the hushed assurance came out of Tuck's mouth, Marion let out a gasp of horror.

Robin's ankle had twisted as a hidden tree root tripped him forward. The lunge he'd aimed for Gisburne had missed. The sound Albion made, as its blade scraped along the edge of Gisburne's weapon, was both shrill and splintering, as the outlaw sank forward.

Will got ready to spring, but Robin had been expecting it, and shouted, 'No Scarlet' as, twisting around a second before his knees hit the ground, Robin hurled himself forwards and swung his sword upwards and sideways, smacking it hard against Gisburne's side.

The force of the blow made Guy stagger, but it helped Robin regain his composure. Ignoring the pain in his ankle, Robin swung Albion back.

Following the blade though, he hit Gisburne hard on the back of the head with the flat of the blade.

The growl of protest that shot from Gisburne was guttural as, in the process of trying to break his fall, his sword fell from his sweating palm. Any further protest was cut short as Robin's boot met his back, pitching him to the earth.

The thump of Guy's head, as it hit the same tree root that had almost caused Robin's downfall, sounded abnormally loud in the suddenly silent forest.

Nobody moved.

Robin stood over Gisburne, his breathing heavy, Albion hanging from his fingers, his ankle sore, and his head pounding with the effort of concentrating for so long.

It was a full minute before anyone spoke.

'You ain't gonna finish him off, are ya?' Will was resigned rather than angry as he picked up Gisburne's sword. 'If that was you down there, you'd be dead already.'

'But it isn't me Will, and I'm not Gisburne.'

'You'll have to kill him one day.'

'Maybe.' Robin gave Marion a tired smile. 'But that's my decision. That's the choice I have to make.'

CHAPTER 18

John and Much returned not long after dawn, having left the horse and cart in Wickham on their way home.

Bleary eyed, they took chunks of bread from an equally tired looking Tuck, as Will, Robin and Marion shuffled from where they'd been asleep, and moved to fire.

There was no disguising the slight limp in Robin's right leg.

Feeling John's unspoken enquiry, Robin explained about the fight with Gisburne. 'It's only a sprain.'

Little John wasn't sure if he was disappointed or relieved that he'd missed the showdown. Although he hadn't been surprised that Robin hadn't killed Guy when he'd had the chance, John had raised

160

his eyebrows when he'd learned that they'd left Gisburne where he'd fallen. His skull cracked; his senses temporarily absent from the world.

In the past they'd have taken him prisoner, or at least put him on a horse and made sure he'd got back to Nottingham. But, this time, he'd been left alone to take his chances against any other passing outlaws or thieves, or even any passing forester or the sheriff's men.

'Nasir is watching over him.'

Much was shocked. 'Gisburne is *still* lying there?'

'Nasir will tell us when he gets back.' Robin watched the flicker of the fire as he spoke. 'I want to know where he goes when he wakes up. If Guy goes back to Nottingham, then our fears that he could be part of these new knights could be wrong and we can concentrate on keeping the people of Sherwood safe during the interdict.'

Tuck tutted as he crossed himself, 'Interdict! Just an excuse for the Pope to throw his weight around!'

Robin agreed, but his thoughts were still on Nottingham. 'You all know Gisburne. He could simply be enjoying making people wonder if he's involved with this mysterious knightly cult, when he's nothing of the sort.'

Marion wasn't so sure. 'He had a tunic though, Robin. Black, with yellow on it.'

'Could have stolen it.' Will scrubbed his hands over his face as he struggled to wake up.

'He could.' Robin looked up at his friends, 'But I think we should keep an extra eye on him for a while, just in case his posturing isn't simply attention-seeking this time.' He got to his feet. 'I'll go and relieve Nasir soon. If Gisburne goes anywhere other than Nottingham when he comes round, then we may have serious cause to worry.'

Buckling on his sword belt, Robin looked up at John. 'Thank you for taking Jerrard home. How is he?'

Little John had only got as far as reporting that Jerrard was being well cared for by his father's personal physician, when Robin spun round to the left. Will and John pulled their swords as the felt someone approach, only to sigh in relief as Nasir strode in.

'He's awake.'

'You followed him?' Robin's hand stayed on Albion as he asked, 'Nottingham or elsewhere?'

'The castle.' Nasir gave Tuck a polite dip of the head as he offered him a cup of ale. 'Gisburne got up, cursed your name, and walked very slowly back to Nottingham.'

Robin exhaled slowly. 'Perhaps he *was* just playing at being important…'

'Or perhaps he wasn't,' Marion muttered. 'At least we know where he is.'

'He is changed.' Nasir sounded wary. 'Battlefields make all men different.'

'Could it just be that?' Robin turned to Will, 'You fought in France, Scarlet. Could that have altered Guy to simply be more… more..?'

'Ruthless?' Marion suggested.

'And he seemed colder.' Tuck added. 'Something I wouldn't have believed possible!'

A shadow crossed Will's face. 'It could. No question.'

Marion hugged Will to her side as she asked, 'What should we do now, Robin? Watch the castle?'

'We'll take a shift each to watch the main gate, see if any guests come to the castle that we don't recognise.'

'Any knights dressed in black and yellow?' Much asked.

Robin was grave, 'If that is their colours. Like we said, Guy could just have pinched a tunic from someone more important than him and fancied pretending he was them for a while. He wouldn't have wanted Flynn telling the sheriff about that, would he. He'd be humiliated. Guy has never taken humiliation kindly.'

'That's true.' Little John gave another massive yawn. 'If you're thinking of heading off to watch Nottingham, Robin, I should tell you the rest of the news from Huntingdon first.'

'Of course.' Robin nodded. 'Sorry, John. Go ahead.'

'It was your father, who came to find us in the woods behind Huntingdon castle. He had a message for you.'

'My father came into the forest to see you himself?'

'He did.' Much beamed. 'He was really nice to us.'

'Good.' Robin wondered why he was surprised that the earl should be kind to his friends when he'd never shown them hostility before. 'The message?'

John rubbed his beard, as if the act helped him to think. 'It was these words precisely. I've been repeating them all the way home so I didn't forget them.'

'He has an' all.' Much rolled his eyes. 'Been driving me mad repeating himself, over an' over and…'

Trying not to show his impatience, Robin repeated, 'The message, John?'

'Right, lad.' John closed his eyes to concentrate.

'Tell my son I want to talk to him, that Jerrard speaks sense, and that he is, and always will be, Mathilda's son—and mine.'

Marion, who'd been wrapping a strip of material around Robin's ankle to help support it, smiled, 'That's good. Will you go to Huntingdon after all?'

Robin pointed to his wounded ankle. 'He could come here.'

Little John patted friend on the shoulder. 'He bids us go to Huntingdon, Robin. With the interdict, he is expecting a hoard of complaining clerics on his doorstep any minute. He wants to make his peace with you while he can.'

A scowl of suspicion clouded Robin's eyes. 'And if I go to *him*, it'll be easier to have one last try at persuading me to stay in Huntingdon.'

'I don't think so. He just wants to talk…' John felt troubled. He was sure Robin would have been pleased that the earl wanted to speak with him, but perhaps not after all. 'Your father said Jerrard was right. What was he right about?'

'I'm sorry John, that's between my father and I.' Robin gave him an apologetic shrug. 'I know I ought to go, but I can't. Herne's warning was clear. If we leave Sherwood unguarded now, it might not just be Gisburne getting away with murder.'

Will, who'd been listening to the exchange with ill-concealed puzzlement, still frustrated that Robin had let Gisburne live, couldn't stand it anymore and let forth a tirade…

'What the hell is it you do want, Robin? First, you want to be reconciled with your father, and then you don't. John and Much go all the way to Huntingdon and back, at breakneck speed, just to deliver your old servant to see your father, then act like they've made your life more complicated on purpose! And why are you so worried about Gisburne killing Flynn? For once, that lousy deputy did us a favour! One less of the sheriff's men has gotta be good, right? Flynn was getting too keen on outlaw-hunting for my liking.'

Robin didn't speak, somewhat taken aback.

'Will's right about Flynn.' Marion looked up at Robin as she finished securing his bandage. 'But Jerrard was right too. We don't know how long it's going to be before the trouble Herne talked of will come. It could be weeks. Apart from the fact that these new knights are mixed up with the church, and may or may not be connected with a few missing noblemen, we know nothing about them at all. You *have* to see your father. You know you do.

'But Sherwood was trying to keep me here. I'm sure of it. And Herne said…'

'I know what Herne said, Robin.' Marion wiped a hair from his forehead. 'But what do *you* say? You may have already made a choice, but now you have to make a decision.'

'You sounded like Herne then, Marion!' smiled Much.

'Marion's right, though,' Robin said, as he turned to John. 'Forgive me, I didn't mean to be ungrateful. I'll do as my father wishes. At least then I will have tried one more time—maybe one last time—to put things right between us. Can you borrow the cart from Meg again? This ankle could do with resting. I'll go today.'

Much, who wasn't entirely sure he knew what was going on, anxiously asked, 'You will come back, won't you, Robin?'

'Yes, Much. I'll always come back.'

Will stood up, 'I think we should all go.'

Robin placed both hands on Will's shoulders. 'No, Will. Thank you, but I need you here. Call me selfish if you like, perhaps I am, but I can only leave if I know that Sherwood is well protected.'

Lowering his head, Will mumbled, 'Well, stay safe, then. And don't be long.'

'Can you sort out watching the castle?'

'We will.' Nasir bowed.

'And if anything happens, I'll borrow a horse and come after you.' John stretched his arms over his head as he gave another cavernous yawn. 'But right now, I'll go back to Wickham and fetch the cart.'

'Thanks, John.'

As Little John picked up his quarterstaff, ready to head back to Meg, Marion slipped a hand into Robin's. 'Can I come to Huntingdon with you? I'd like to.'

'My own Mathilda.' Robin kissed the tip of Marion's nose. 'I'd like that. I'd like that very much.'

EPILOGUE

Tuck dropped the bag of bread and wrapped venison he'd been preparing for Robin and Marion to take to Huntingdon. Seizing his staff, he backed into the trees. Will Scarlet was at his side. The friar watched the rise and fall of his chest as, with a sword in one hand and a knife in the other, Will stared into the forest.

On the opposite side of the camp, Tuck could just see Much and Marion, their bows already drawn. Robin and Nasir had completely disappeared, merging with the trees the moment they'd collectively heard the sound of running feet.

Two seconds later, Tuck sagged with relief as two familiar figures bounded into the camp.

Little John, followed by a panting Edward of Wickham, didn't waste time apologising for the lack of cart, or putting for their friends on their guard with such a noisy arrival.

'Tell them, Edward.' John pushed the head of Wickham villager forward. 'Tell them.'

Catching his breath, Edward wiped a hand over his mouth, his face grey as his words raced from his lips. 'The interdict has been announced.'

'So soon?' Robin saw Tuck cross himself.

'Soldiers are already watching the churches. They're demanding all the keys and locking the church doors.' Edward looked shaken. 'The villagers in Wickham are afraid, Robin.'

'As I'm sure everyone in the country is.' Robin looked at Marion, her face had paled. 'Edward, has anyone mentioned any knights or anything about an apocalypse?'

'Apocalypse? No. Nothing like that.' Edward shook his head, 'But a knight has gone missing from the manor near Edwinstowe. The Lord's eldest son. I don't know his name. Father Michael sent a messenger to tell us about the interdict, he told us of the missing man too.'

'Something is coming. Follow your heart as brother fights brother and the kingdom shakes...' Robin closed his eyes, as he muttered to himself, 'The sons must choose as the Apocalypse rides.'

Marion exchanged a worried glance with her friends. 'Robin?'

Robin's eyes flew back open. 'Edward, you must get back to Wickham. Prepare everyone for tough times ahead. We may not be around to help you as much as we would like for a while.' Switching his attention to Nasir, he said, 'Go to Nottingham with Much. Watch the main gates to the town and the castle. If *any* knights, nobles or churchmen of rank visit de Rainault, then we need to know.'

'You aren't going to Huntingdon, then?' Scarlet was watching the trees, as if he expected a cohort of black clad enemies to burst through the branches.

'Unfortunately, my father will have to wait.'

Marion slipped a hand into Robin's. 'We'll see him soon. Come on, we don't know if anything bad is going to happen beyond the closing of the churches—do we?'

Robin didn't reply. He could feel the Lord of the Forest's warnings galloping around his head.

Raising Albion to the trees, Robin cried out, 'Herne protect us!'

As the outlaws and Edward echoed Robin's prayer, Will raised his eyes to the sky. A cloud had blown across the sun, obscuring the early morning light. 'Herne was right, wasn't he? Something is coming.'

'Something bad.' Robin thrust Albion back into his belt and stood up straight. His face was set with determination. 'If my instincts can be trusted, Will, I would say that all hell is about to break loose.'[5]

5 This adventure is a direct precursor to *The Knights of the Apocalypse* by Richard Carpenter, available in print, eBook and audio formats.

You may also enjoy…

You may also enjoy…

www.ingramcontent.com/pod-product-compliance
Lightning Source LLC
Chambersburg PA
CBHW011501170626
46814CB00008B/2997